Junction Book

JUNCTION BOOK

A MYSTERY GONE OFF THE RAILS

BY

KEN NEWTON,
ANN BALL
AND
WILLIAM NEW

First printing 2015

ISBN   979-1-77221-003-3

eISBN 978-1-77221-005-7

Issued also in print and electronic formats.
ISBN 978-1-77221-003-3 (pbk.).--ISBN 978-1-77221-005-7 (pdf)
        I. Ball, Ann, 1954-, author II. New, William, 1959-, author
III. Title.

PS8627.E963J86 2015   C813'.6   C2015-900775-5
                                      C2015-900776-3

Leaping Lion Books Publishing
4700 Keele Street
Toronto, ON M3J 1P3

www.yorku.ca/llbooks/

We dedicate this book to our parents.

No matter what you do
No matter where you go
You've got to have an ace in the hole

Table of Contents

November 13, 1951   1
Gaak—Will
Danger—Red
Walking to the Metropole—Red
Double R—Al
Lost Will and Testimony—Red
Metropole Summit Number One—Red

November 14, 1951   32
Al Again—Al
Talking with the Union—Red
BBC—Will
Number Nine—Red
Night at the Ballet—Will
Once More—Al
Metropole Summit Number Two—Will

November 15, 1951   68
Lucky Strike—Al
Stake out at the Old Corral—Red
Nakev—Al
Mulled It Over Some —Will
Kat—Al
No Movement at Number Thirteen—Red
Preacher Jack—Al
Man of the Hour—Will

November 16, 1951   103
Metropole Summit Number Three—Al
Before and After Summit Number Three—Red

"Squire . . ." He Said Pleasantly—Will
Tempest in a Teapot—Al
Talking with Sarah—Red
Message for Mr. O—Al
We Watched Him Go—Will
An Evening Well Spent—Al
Metropole Summit Number Four—Red

November 17, 1951   **134**
Gunshot—Al
I'm Here If You Need Me—Al
If I Knew You Were Coming . . . —Red
Metropole Summit Number Five—Red

November 18, 1951   **157**
It is Sunday . . . Yawn!—Al
Aim for the Blur—Red

November 19, 1951   **164**
It Seems I've Heard That Song Before—Al
Black Cats Creep Across My Path—Red
And The People Start to Sing—Al
A Cold Night with A Purple Sky—Red
Metropole Summit Number Six—Al

November 20, 1951   **185**
I Don't Like Surprises—Al

Afterword   **193**

Acknowledgements   **195**

NOVEMBER 13, 1951

GAAK—WILL'S VERSION

It was first thing in the morning—noon—and I was at my desk reading The Tely. I was just catching up with Edwin Boyd's latest exploits when the call came in.

Cursing the interruption (I'd been following Edwin and the robberies as if it were my favourite radio play), I spilled my coffee and Seagram's 83 trying to reach the phone before a second shrill ring.

Waves of nausea lapped at the shore of my pained morning after. I swallowed hard against the rising bile and managed to make a sound that was half grunt, half something like, "Hello?"

"Jones! You reprobate . . . Jeez, you sound like death warmed up. No need to ask how you're doing, obviously."

I smiled through my pain. A kind of rictus that was automatic when talking to almost anyone from the old

1

neighbourhood—Smith and I went way back. We both came from the wrong side of the tracks running through the West Toronto Junction—one of those places where both sides of the tracks are wrong. The connection had bad static, like he was calling from Paris an ocean away, instead of the three or four miles that it was.

"Gaak," was all I could manage to say.

"Hello!" he yelled. I heard a sound like he was slamming the phone on something, probably his typewriter.

"This is important, goddammit. Pull up your socks, I might have something for you," he said, a bit calmer.

"Roy?" I managed. Still wobbly, but more like speech. "What's that about my socks?" I was genuinely puzzled.

"Right," he began, ignoring me. "You remember Mr. O? Mr. O, small time bookie, works over by you?"

"Yeah. I know him. He's not even that small. By far the main action in the Junction. He's just quiet, that's all."

"Well, maybe not so quiet anymore. His youngest boy turned up shot out west somewhere."

"No kidding? Junior? I know him. Wait. Shot how bad?"

"Now it's like you used to know him. Look, I know the kid's mother, Mr. O's wife. Don't ask how I know her . . . . She called, naturally upset about the kid but mad too about the rigmarole she's getting."

"Could put it down to a mother grieving for her boy cut down too young and all that."

"No, I thought of that, and also that these people in general don't like the police, as can only be expected, given the nature of making book vis-à-vis, its contrary aspect to the laws of the fair burg. But the old broad has a legitimate beef. The cops are arguing jurisdiction—oh yeah, I should tell you, they found the kid in Winnipeg."

"What? Winnipeg?"

"Yes. Try to keep up! They found him in Winnipeg, out west in a refrigerated freight car, filled with mostly beef to keep Junior company. But here's the thing: where do you think the train started from? From our old stomping grounds . . . "

"Where? You mean the—?"

"Yup," he cut me off. "The Junction. Innarrested?"

"You came to the right place," I lied, reaching for what Dot Parker would call the office pen. "What else you got? Maybe start with where I can reach Junior's old doll."

"No can do, boy-o. She wants me to handle this from her end. Under no circumstances are you to get in touch with her—she'll play absolute mute if you do."

"Absolute mute?" I bit my lip so as not to laugh. Roy was always making up expressions that he thought sounded like something a jazz musician might say. "Mute is an absolute. You can't be just a little bit mute."

"Absolute dumb, then. If you go to her, she'll play absolute dumb. You can be a little dumb, right?"

"Clearly." I bit my lip again, but this time the laugh got by me.

"Funny. Okay, you and yer partners can look at this for me. Let's call it 10 days at yer rate—a double saw a day, right?"

"Plus expenses."

"Right. So two hundred dollars plus expenses, a hundred of which you still owe me on the series. Did you hear DiMaggio might be retiring? Well, rumour has it anyways. You'll never get any of that dough back. Old Joe sure dinged you a few times, didn't he? You should give up betting on baseball games. Eddie Gaedel would prob'ly go four for four if you bet on the other team."

"Listen, Smith. My partners won't like that about the hundred. Al's not gonna wanna pay off my gambling debts."

"So pad the expenses a bit. No way I ever see that dough from you. I'm a gonna take it off the top from Junior's mother. Already did in fact."

DANGER—RED'S VERSION

Leaving Will the Kid alone in our office was dangerous if you ask me. On the first day of this awful case, late and hung over, he staggered in smoking an awful hand rolled cigarette. Will grunted something unintelligible in my direction. He turned, lurched out then lurched back into our office 10 minutes later, gripping a coffee which smelled suspiciously sweetened. He swiped Al's Tely and dropped his smoke into the heavy amber ashtray before he dropped himself into a chair. As his palm and long fingers held his head, seemingly keeping it from falling forward, he scanned the headlines. Will made it into the office a minute before noon—an early start for the Kid.

Al, of course, had been in, read The Tely and The Star, made a few calls and left for lunch. Al, unlike the Kid, keeps regular hours and then some more in his firm. An old accountant friend of Al's prospered last year, needed bigger digs and offered us a modest sublease on his former Sterling Tower office. From our office on the 15th floor, we saw Toronto stretch northwards, City Hall and subway construction hopscotch on Yonge Street. With our new Bay Street address and Empire phone suffix, our sleuthing firm, Al Green and Associates—licensed and bonded—took on a respectable air. Well, respectable until the sublease dries up next year. The office was small for the three of us, but rarely would we all be in at the same time. Al and Will shared their desk, thank goodness for tender mercies. Only the Metropole's bartender, Bruno, knew the hotel's beer parlour was our real headquarters. Al was there for lunch. He invited me to join him after Will dropped into the office. No need to mention, Al is an optimist.

I decided to attempt communication with Will.

"Will."

Grunt.

"You okay?"

Oink.

"Need anything?"

Wheeze.

"Would you look after the phone for an hour or so?"

"Ahh . . . ohhh."

Frustrated, I queried, "May I set you on fire with a blow torch?"

"Take the Seagram's out of my pocket first," Will may have mumbled into the paper.

"Just checking to see if you're alive. I'm heading to the Metropole to meet Al. Don't do anything I wouldn't do. If the phone rings, say 'Hello.' Be courteous. Take notes, including the phone number," I said with a loud, slow emphasis on the last phrase.

"Yeah, ma'am," Will the Kid uttered the most hated

of his stock phrases.

"I'll ma'am ya," I said and threw a notepad, missing his head but clattering in the ribboned venetian blinds. I heard a strange snort-like noise before slamming the door.

Shortly after I made the mistake of leaving and heading down Bay, Will picked up another lousy case from the Junction. His old buddy Roy Smith, made deals with everyone on the sly and on the cheap. Another Junction whodunit. This time with a body.

WALKING TO THE METROPOLE–RED'S VERSION

Never mind Will. For one glorious moment, I was blissfully unaware of Will's conversation and our new case.

When Susan, one of the four blond elevator attendants, wished me a "Good day, miss," I felt thankful for our most recent lucky break: our new office. The Sterling office was cooler digs than the one we had on Yonge Street, a walk up over Yamada's Photo Studio, with cooler guys hanging around too. Sterling Tower boasts 21 floors, working staffed elevators and a marbled lobby. Out the double doors, I turned my coat collar up against the cold drizzle of the brownish day and breathed out against the soft envelope of the city's contaminated air. The stench of auto exhaust, coal dust, oil fumes and the construction grit trapped by low clouds made downtown Toronto smell almost as bad as the stockyards these days. Well, 'as bad' is an exaggeration. Nothing in this sweet Dominion smells or feels as bad as the stockyards. I'll take the exhaust, dust, fumes and grit over the slaughterhouse stench and diesel ash any day. Al and Will, with their go-as-you-please maliciousness, gleefully walked me around their old Junction neighbourhood three years ago. When I started with Al's firm, I had no idea how many of our cases would originate from the source of Toronto's nickname, Hogtown. Inescapably, our stockyard cases turned into those "good news, bad news" stories, sorta like Al Green and Will Jones themselves.

Once on King, the Ladies and Escorts door of the Metropole came to view. A tiny older woman, with her nylons rolled up to her bowlegged knees, and her hat pulled slightly above her eyes fixed me with a stare and said, "You're on the road to hell." Cheery. She looked as if she knew what she was talking about. Ignoring her, I soldiered on and pushed through the wooden door.

"Hey Bruno, whatta you know?" I recited to our guy behind the bar.

"I know it's time for you to dump those two losers and for us two to hook up," Bruno replied.

"That'll be the day, Bruno. That'll be the day. Speaking of losers, where's Al?"
He nodded to the back of the parlour. "Usual spot, Red. Where else? 'Cept, he was just yapping on the blower with Will just a minute ago. Sounds like you're up for a doozy. The one that was on the front page for a week or a couple now. What'd they say? Gone west, young man. Too bad he was dead in a box car." Bruno's quips were often deadpan.

"Thanks for the tip." I said.

Bruno turned his attention to the bar as I turned and strode to the back of the parlour. Another "good news, bad news" story. I cursed under my breath. I did leave Will alone, so the fault was mine. If I had eaten breakfast this morning, I might have waited for Al to return from lunch. I could have mediated the call, and Will would be content with his sweet coffee and paper. Yet hope battled regret over leaving: maybe Bruno was pulling my leg. Maybe Al had reined Will in this time. Maybe Will forgot the number, or imagined the call. I let out a deep breath. Maybe some cows sprouted wings and flew to greener pastures.

I saw Al scribbling away in his notebook at our table. His shoulders were hunched and his head hung over the page. His arms were a little too long for the shirt he was wearing. His legs stretched out into the aisle as the chair legs were too short for his frame. Tall, fair and handsome, Al's good humour showed in his facial expressions. As I pulled my chair back, he said without looking up, "What took you so long? Stop at Woolworth's on the way?"

"Cut it out, Al. I know you talked to Will," I bluffed as I remained standing.

"I talk with Will. I talk with you. I talk with Bruno. Bruno with the big ears and even bigger mouth, it seems. Ahh, our messy cases. Red, Red, Red . . . these cases are part of life. Part of the biz, yes?" Al played it light. He leaned back in his chair as he scratched his temple, raised his eyebrows and smiled his half smile. He'd just confirmed what I'd bluffed.

"Part of the biz? Part of life? Allowing Will to pick up cases? He could barely walk and talk when he came in this morning. Are you going to tell me that Will took on the investigation of a bookmaker's son's murder?

8

From who? The bookmaker, gamblers, the cops? This thing's a stinking mess. The cops aren't interested. The Winnipeg Police and the RCMP are kicking it. The paper put the story front page, right? Toronto the Good faints at the exposure of its undercarriage. What's worse is it's still just another stinking Junction case. This is part of life? How's this stench a part of our life?" I wasn't stomping my square heels, but I was close to it.

Al stared for a long minute before speaking.

"Lower your nose, Red. It may be another stinking Junction case—as you say—but it's also part of our biz. You got anything lined up to pay the bills? Well, Will does."

I felt the temperature rise from my neck, and my cheeks blazed. My old friend, a tenant down the hall from me at the Lloyd George, became a reluctant client. Pam Esson had sober second thoughts about locating her layabout father.

I regretted saying the word "stinking" in conjunction with the word "Junction." Al was protective about his old neighbourhood and he did not appreciate speeches set to the tap of heels. I hated when Al scored a point and deemed my objection irrational. It was unfair that the financial point trumped my rational point every time. I already knew, that even before we three met about the case , I was going to be outvoted on whether or not we take it. I slumped into the chair and into silence.

I did not care who is lining up the jobs. I hated the stinking stockyards.

"Look Red, Will will be here in five. Let's talk the whole thing over when he gets here. What'd you eat today? Nothing? I thought so. Shepherd's pie is on the board, let's split it and I'll buy you a shandy too." As usual, Al tried his best to move everything along. Al hailed the waiter, John, who nodded back that he would come around.

A minute or two later I heard a chair being knocked over, and a loud curse somewhere behind me, signalling the arrival of Will the Kid. He poured himself into the chair beside us like mercury; fluidity in motion is Will. His cigarette had gone out and he was distractedly patting himself down for matches. Al tossed his lighter at him. Will caught it, lit the roll-your-own and pitched the lighter back. Uck. The scent of crappy tobacco. John brought the pie divided on two plates, a shandy, two King's Plates and a Seagram's blue jug filled with water. The water would go untouched. John knew the importance of his customers' stock orders and of a civil appearance.

Will recounted his conversation with Roy Smith from Hagar Avenue, noting the street to jog Al's memory. Roy called on behalf of a distraught Mrs. O and to finish his report, Will recited Smith's phone number, digit by digit. I could brain him sometimes. We agreed that a quick poke around the neighbourhood this afternoon would help us decide whether to officially take the case. Al said he'd check out the neighbourhood and Will and I were to visit the ice house, presumably where the body was loaded onto the boxcar. We would meet back here for dinner. The brat in me queried if anyone noticed today is November 13th. Will countered that it did not count, because today is Tuesday, not Friday. With this news, Al stood, nodded at John, plunked down two one-dollar bills and said, "Let's go."

The meeting was over.

DOUBLE R–AL'S VERSION

On a corner at Maria Street, I studied what we called The Garlic, a small theatre on the corner of Gilmour Avenue and Dundas Street West. My mother visited every Tuesday and, for an additional 10 cents, received a plate or some other piece of a dish set. Women from all over the greater Junction area did the same and Harry, the sole usher they employed, knew almost all of them by name. Not by first name, of course, as that would be considered impolite: "Hello, Mrs. Newton . . . Mrs. Cohen . . . Mrs. Sebarras . . . Mrs. Green . . . " From the corner, I glimpsed the bookmaker's office where nothing seemed to be happening. Not a surprise, as the thoroughbred races at Dufferin were extended two days because of bad weather. What should have concluded Thursday would now end with the Saturday race card, and that would be the last race day until spring.

I heard the door of the Maria Street Mission slam and turned to see Preacher Jack step toward the street, smiling as he recognized a familiar face. He was a big man. His hair was thinning, but he was still a strong blond. We hadn't seen each other for quite a few years, and while his warm demeanour remained unchanged, worry lines marked his round face. "I heard you're investigating that young man's unfortunate death."

Despite the topic, he was beaming with recognition, delighted to see me even though he couldn't yet recall my name. I nodded, keeping my opinion of the boy to myself. I'd be hard-pressed to call the matter unfortunate,

11

as the boy was far from a saint. In fact, he was such a rotten son-of-a-bitch, the number of likely candidates increased tenfold. The reverend didn't pick up on my thoughts but admitted that he really couldn't be of any assistance as he really didn't know the "poor boy."

"Perhaps the neighbours might help," he said nodding to the street. He was alluding to the fact that the murdered boy was Jewish and I might find out something about him at the Junction Shul.

"Worth a try," I said. "Got time for coffee or something?"

I expected him to beg off but he must have been hungry and agreed to a quick bite. We ended up in the Double R. The electoral riding of High Park had been dry since 1904, probably would exercise its local option for a long time to come, as the city ordained that High Park could go wet if 60 percent of the voters cast their ballots in favour of a reversal. There was no chance of embarrassing him by lunching in an establishment where they served liquor. Well, at least over the counter.

Over lunch, I got a pretty thorough update of family life on our side of the tracks and a few scraps of information that might help us understand the killer's motive and identity. General knowledge had it that the old man and his youngest hadn't been getting along for a few months. In addition, his two elder brothers had become publicly angry with Junior over whatever it was that had been getting up the old man's nose.

Before we left, George Stravroff dropped by our table to ask how we liked his spiffed- up place. A happy reunion of sorts. When I was a kid, George sponsored our football team and the preacher our softball and hockey teams. Although many just called the preacher "Jack" or "Reverend Jack." I called him all three, depending on the conversation.

As Preacher Jack strolled to the Imperial Bank on the corner to discuss what he called "church business," I mused his everlasting overdraft was also general knowledge. With 15 minutes before the bank closed, his stroll was more a quick step. Watching him while standing in front of Guffin's Hardware store, I could picture the Runnymede-Dundas streetcar coming out of the loop to its first stop. My mother and I stood on this spot for our December trips to Eaton's Toyland. The old orange and black sign was still in place: 27 Minutes to City Hall.

I wondered how Preacher Jack knew that the thing bothering the two eldest sons was the same thing that also bothered the old man. The family wasn't open about their business. How might Jack know about the feud? Also, he said he had heard I was investigating the young man's death. So soon? From whom? Our decision to look into the murder was only hours old. For the reverend to know, either Red or Will telephoned while I traveled west on the Dundas-Runnymede streetcar, or Roy's been thinking out loud. Curious.

The big man's office and factory building was also on the corner of Dundas and Gilmour, cater-corner from The Garlic. From the moment I had heard the door of the Mission slam behind me, I knew Mr. O was watching from the third floor of that building. One of his family had been murdered. He would take an interest in everything that went on around him until he knew who was responsible and that the guilty party had been dealt with.

The third floor was where the active bookmaking operation was conducted. A big betting parlour, as it were, but with the Ontario tracks dark there wasn't enough action from the eastern American tracks to keep the big room open. What's more, the time difference made any handle the west might generate a losing proposition. Standardbred racing would be starting at Dufferin, but the action would be lighter. Raids by the cops from the Keele Street station took place during this period, which caused the man on the street to nod his head knowingly.

I deliberately crossed Dundas Street, heading north toward Maria Street, so his line of sight was cut by the buildings along the north side. I passed the Runnymede Pharmacy and Dempsey's hole-in-the-wall Canadian Pacific Railway Lunch. Between the two places, I realized the old Cole Porter song Ace In The Hole was running through my mind off and on and had been since we talked about this job. It wasn't just because the lyrics mentioned the hotel Metropole, our favourite watering hole. Red liked the Ladies and Escorts room, but also appreciated the fact that she could just walk into the main room anytime and nobody paid any attention—well, let us say nobody got out of line. I had never been sure of the right words to that song. I knew it really didn't mean our Metropole but it engendered a feeling of affinity all the same. I resolved once again to ask the habitués of the pump room to enlighten me as to the correct words.

After Blore's Taxi office, I passed the "long store," so-called by all and sundry. It was very long and not very deep. It sold all the things that variety stores would eventually come to handle so you didn't have to go to the corner grocery store and mingle with the old ladies waiting to get the entrée for their old man's dinner, or a mickey of rye, or a package of prophylactics or some other personal item. As I got to the door, Cappie stepped out onto the street, unwrapping the cellophane wrapper of a panatella. He was heavier than he had been when I first knew him. Aren't we all?

His smile displayed a set of white teeth, his eyes the glint of recognition. "Raschi. I haven't seen you for a long while. You moving back into the old neighbourhood?"

I swung my head gently back and forth, conveying a soft negative response. With the word Raschi, Cappie had taken me back to my baseball-playing days. When playing sandlot ball, most infielders would take a turn pitching batting practice to strengthen their throwing arms. He, as a spectator, would yell words of encouragement, and never used my real name. I don't think he knew my real name. He called out Raschi. Anyone who knew anything at all about baseball knew Vic Raschi as he, Allie Reynolds and Eddie Lopat were leading the Yankees to another World Series.

"You're nosing around the murder, eh?" he said, more of a statement than a question.

"Yah!" I used my best local accent. "What's your take on it?"

"You're getting paid and I ain't but you're going to pick my brain, right?"

"Look Cappie, I know the Maria Street Dark Boys are mindful of their turf. Somebody local getting wasted does not go unnoticed. You got the skinny on the hit or no? "

"No."

There was a pause while he lit the cigar and enjoyed

the first full drag. "We can make a deal," he said. "The old man knows you're working on this and he is not going to get in your way."

I looked him straight in the eye. "We are not working this case. A couple of hours ago, we agreed to evaluate the possibility but everybody seems to believe that we are working the case. Somebody take out an ad in the dailies?"

The verve was back in his eyes as he took another drag on that foul smelling thing. "Mr. O's wife had an associate call you people and arrange a deal. He called us in to police things up and told us you would be looking at it from your angle. We talked to the reverend Jack because the deceased had an eye for the young lady who does all the Mission's secretarial work. Mind you, he had an eye for any broad under fifty."

"And?" I asked.

"And what?" Cappie said.

"He had an eye for Kat who no longer qualifies as a young lady," I waited expectantly.

"Yeah. Middle-aged." he said.

Handing him one of our Green and Associates' cards, I asked how I could reach him. "Call the Double R and leave a message with George. I'll get back to you when I can." We left it at that. I jumped on a Dundas car for the Metropole with Will and Red.

The damn tune was running through my mind again. What was it about that tune?

LOST WILL AND TESTIMONY—RED'S VERSION

Will wanted to make a telephone call and pick up a

strip of streetcar tickets. All the way to Sterling Tower, he argued we should travel by the St. Clair Avenue West streetcar. We would travel through different neighbourhoods than the ones on the Dundas car and, if we got lucky, we might pick up a tip coming into the Junction from another part of town. I waited in the marble lobby and grabbed the tickets while Will made a call. Luck was with us as the Yonge bus came quickly and detoured off Yonge Street. The wait for the St. Clair connection did not bother Will—he had cigarettes—but something else was. Considering the streetcar loop at Keele Street, we would have to march along a good stretch of St. Clair Avenue West before reaching the ice house. Will was quiet about it, but he hated walking past those damn plants and animal pens almost as much as I did.

I jumped onto the St. Clair car and the driver—a heavy-set, middle-aged man in a carefully pressed dark blue suit with a cap—sweetly greeted me, but gave Will the gears and held the car to examine his transfer. "You related to the Hatteys?" the driver asked.

"Nope."

"The Littles?"

"Nay."

"O'Learys?"

"Noooo."

Struggling to place Will's family, the driver relented and abandoned his pastime of pinpointing passengers in his neighbourhood and finally let Will aboard. The Kid slumped in the seat across from me and looked out the window like he was dreaming. The glass was clouded with the cold fighting the damp.

Along St. Clair street, I noted the driver's relationship

with his regulars. Men and women alike greeted him by his name, Frank, and chit-chatted with him about their outing or clucked about the sleety, cold weather. One rider thanked him profusely for holding the car last week when he was running late for work. That was the day before the big storm. If he missed the streetcar, he would be out of work when he walked in the plant.

Somewhere around Lansdowne, near Prospect Cemetery, a guy with a green coat boarded the car much to Frank's delight. Old, old war buddies, I surmised from the patter over the fare box. Mr. Green Coat questioned loudly if anyone aboard spoke 'frog' and when no one spoke up, breathed an exaggerated sigh of relief and led the car in a rousing rendition of "It's a Long Way to Tipperary." Will, with his eyes closed, looked like he was about to vomit. I thought to myself, remember this scene for the next time he suggests an alternate transportation route to the Dundas steady ride. After singing, Mr. Green Coat delivered a heartfelt speech incorporating pieces about the glory of Canada, the pomp of His Majesty's ordination and the importance of tradition, in case anyone needed the lessons.

"The greatest land of all lands is the land where we live," Mr. Green Coat testified to streetcar passengers and in response, received a hearty applause and laughter. Live theatre for under a dime. Even less for us, since the office buys books of tickets.

We travelled the hundred yards down to the route's final loop. Even with the steady rain, a rancid smell seeped through the cracks. Shoot me dead, we were back by those horrid plants, unloaded on the eastern edge of the stockyards. Thankfully, the rain tempered the rail yard and incinerator soot. People said goodbye as they filed by our driver, Frank, and our serenader, Mr. Green Coat, at the front of the car. Umbrellas snapped when unfurled. I ventured towards the front while Will slipped out the back doors for a smoke.

"Thanks for the ride, Frank. May I call you Frank?" I smiled.

"Sure, young lady, surely you can for that's my name." Frank said.

"I am Sean. What may we call you?" piped up Green Coat.

"Everybody calls me Red. That'll do."

"You sure they don't call you 'Freckles'?" Green Coat continued to annoy.

"No."

Frank told me to ignore the old coot and asked where I was from. I told him he would not know the small place north of Kingston, since even the locals do not know what it's called. When Frank laughed, I started asking about Junior before he tried to direct the conversation any further:

"Anyway, Frank, you know everybody. That Junction guy, Junior, who was found shot up in Winnipeg, did he ride this car?" I began. As Al taught me, offering a reason for posing such a question is unnecessary. People are natural snoops and gossips, especially in front of a receptive audience.

"Nah, he drove the old man's Studebaker every-where," said Frank. "One of the boys from the yard said he'd see him walking along St. Clair or Dundas from time to time. People are talking about Junior though. Nothing like a local murder to break the tedium. Some of the guys got it solved. Somebody yesterday said he knew for a fact that one of those robbers who broke out of the Don Jail did it. The main robber once drove the bus route on Yonge, did you know that? Anyway, people dream up the craziest ideas. I think some guys had run-ins with Junior as he collected bets for his old man, but the guys don't talk with me about their gambling. They know I'd turn 'em in or give 'em a piece of my mind. Or, worse still, turn Fred here on 'em."

Mr. Fred Green Coat rolled his eyes and shrugged with an exaggerated innocence, "What! What!" He acted out Jerry Lewis' goofy guy imitation.

"Thanks Frank. Know anything else about Junior?" I asked.

"Well, police were around last Friday asking a question or two, but, according to the guys, they aren't breaking a sweat and spent more time bellyaching about doing the RCMP's job. Anyway, his old man's taking it bad I hear, but his mother, worse . . . Look, Red, I gotta go. People need me to get where they're going. Yah sure you want off here?"

"Yeah, I do, and, yeah, I don't. Thanks for asking, Frank." As I stepped off the car, I heard Mr. Green Coat sing the refrain from Hey, Good Looking and Frank's laughter followed by a chastisement, "Leave the kid alone."

"Get anything?" Will asked as the streetcar pulled off.

"Nothing hard, but there's a lot of gossip. Some of the guys had run-ins with Junior because they were welching on their bets. Maybe somebody getting him back knocked him off? Also, police showed up with a couple of questions but haven't been around since last

Friday. Nothing we didn't guess."

We started up towards St. Clair; me walking with my umbrella and Will with a turned up collar. My associates taught me a handkerchief held to one's mouth or nose is considered bad manners in the stockyards. I knew this, but every time I came back here, I wondered how people live and work with the stench without wearing gas masks. However, as suggested by Al and Will, I breathed through my mouth to help me cope with the smell of manure from the pens and vats of fat, mixed with bone and blood of meat slabs from Swift's and Canada Packer's. All those farm animals, railroaded to this place in Toronto for the killing, packing and hauling. That's what the stockyards smelled like to me, endless killing and packing. I would have dropped onto the sidewalk but the trodden bits beneath my feet prevented me from the crawl.

Just a quick march past the jutted loading docks and brownish buildings of Swift's and the old Gunn's plants, we turned right at the truck entrance to the ice house. The Kid and I turned up the gated road and made our way up to a dead end. The road, dark with dirt, stopped at the ice house. Will and I scanned both sides for anything unusual—signs of scuffle, tire marks, a tossed gun, who knows what—but only saw what one might expect on a private commercial road: 70 feet of weeds, junk, puddles and pot holes. All the while, animal and machinery noise formed the distinct Toronto stockyards refrain.

As we approached the street's end, we saw a lone, lean worker loading ice from the hopper, covered from the rain by an overhang. First, he pushed a steel box the size of a two-by-four-by-six steamer trunk into a vat of hot water, then pulled the box out of the water and pulled the bolt and dumped a smoking block of ice. When the ice pick hit the ice, the block split along the line formed by the indent in the steel box. He picked the broken piece up with tongs and threw it overhead into a five foot cone-shaped hopper on overhead tracks. He repeated this process again and again. Once the hopper was full, he wheeled over the boxcar and dumped the ice through an opening in its roof and slammed the roof door shut. Having observed the guy enough, Will waited then walked closer to the overhang for protection from the rain.

"Hey there!" Will called over to the man at the loading dock.

The lean man looked over his shoulder and, evidently puzzled by the sight of us standing there, turned to reach for another box.

"Hey there . . . time for a smoke, ain't it?" Will played his standard trump. Mr. Lean stopped, turned, and held his fingers toward the Kid.

"How'd yous know?" he drawled. Will handed one up with a couple of wood matches and took one himself. Wretched cigarettes lit, they both inhaled and exhaled like they were breathing in mountain air.

"Yous look kinda lost," Mr. Lean observed.

"My name's Will. This here's Red. You?" The guy remained silent. Will waited a few beats before speaking again. "Me and Red here are looking around 'bout Junior O's murder. Working with the Old Man. You know Junior, the bookie's kid, who turned up dead in Winnipeg . . . the one in the paper a week or so back?"

"Yah, yah, we know Junior," said Mr. Lean. "The cops were here last Friday talking to Max, our boss, about any funny stuff going on with the cars. Spent a long time complaining about the RCMP. Young kid and older guy. Left a card to call . . . Old, something . . . David, no . . . Daniel Old. Constable Daniel Old outta Number Nine, Keele. It's up on the wall inside. Waste of time and a visit. Nobody knows nothing." He stopped talking for another drag.

"Nobody knows nothing?" said Will. "Double negative isn't that? Anyway, is 'nothing' the company version or yours? Even I knew Junior, and I moved outta here five years ago. Junior's the silent but deadly type. Never saw a scrap he didn't like and scrapping was his business. No, that ain't right. Junior loved scrapping beyond the need for it. Hair trigger temper. And you say nobody's heard or seen something?"

"Yah, strange ain't it. But, you're right about the temper. Bert down on the floor got his arm broke by him. Not over a bet, but 'cause Bert accidentally cut Junior off once. Bert was off for a month. Tough on the kids, though the neighbours and Committee chipped in. Real charmer, Junior." Lean took another long drag while looking at Will sorta sideways.

"Bert get over his arm being broke?" Will asked.

"Hey, it ain't like that. Bert got four mouths needing food and knows where his bread is buttered. Knocking off the local bookie's kid don't feed four mouths in the short or the long run. More trouble than it's worth."

"True. Anything else of import?" Will asked.

"Nothing else from us here. No automobiles, no commotion, and no bodies been shoved into a car on my shift. Or on the other two shifts either. I wouda heard if a dead body came up the road and landed in the hopper. But there's one thing kinda strange. I heard through the grapevine, the cops were called out to Ryding Avenue or St. Clair last week and fired off a couple of shots. Some kinda hustle going on."

"What kinda hustle?" said Will.

"Who the hell are yous?" shouted a big fellow with a white hat as he suddenly lurched onto the platform. My guess: Max the manager.
Lean flipped the cigarette out and off the platform and reached for a box as he gets back to work.

"We're looking into Junior's final whereabouts," said Will. "You know anything about him?"

"Who's 'we'? You two his parents?" quipped the suspected Max.

"No, Al Green and Associates. You're looking at the associates, Al's around somewhere. You Max?"

"Yah, I'm Max, Master Associate. And Max wants no associates . . . green, wet or otherwise. I already talked to the cops. Like I said, nothing happened here. Now, shove off my dock. You're on private property. I got ice needs loading." Max inched closer to the edge and to us. It was my time to chime in.

"I know work needs doing, Max. We're leaving. But the problem is the train came from here and ended up in St. Boniface. So did Junior. Dead Junior. Might you take a card in case you hear anything? You might, you're the boss after all." I stepped forward with a shy smile and extended a gift of our card: "If you can't get us there, leave a message at the Double R."

He leaned down and took the card. "I'll stick this

24

card by the other one. Cops know yous?"

"We're just trying to help with this dreadful situation as best as we can," I replied.

"My, my, my. Well. Bye, Miss Florence Nightingale. Bye, Master Associate. By the way, don't get too soaked and don't sit by the phone too long." Max ended the conversation with the turn of his back. Lean cracked another block.

We walked down the lonely road to St. Clair. Out of earshot, I turned to Will.

"Whaddya think, Kid?"

"The shoot out on Ryding caught my attention . . . if it's true."

"Right, I'm thinking the same. Worth a wander over there. Maybe you could ask a few questions." I suggested.

"Might do that, ma'am. Where's Ryding?"

"Jeez, Will. You grew up here, not me. Ask Al, why don't ya?" I stopped and wondered why I fell for his teases.

Changing my tone, I continued.

"Anyway, not much is new other than the gunshots. Junior was the enforcer. Although, Bert's broken arm might be worth a few conversations, I assume Bert cut him off in an automobile? Maybe the nothing-happened-routine is the result of Bert's union brothers deciding to do something about Junior."

There was a long silence.

"Who you working for now, The Tely?" said Will. "Let's see . . . I dunno . . . oh, oh, now I know, the Packinghouse Workers' Organizing Committee did it."

"Stop, Will, just stop. You know what I mean. Junior broke a guy's arm who works on the killing floor. Not an official hit, but you know how the guys look after each other. God knows, nobody else does."

Heading west on St. Clair, we passed the long white pens holding the Holsteins and stopped at Symes Road as drovers with canes drove a herd across St. Clair from the cattle lanes, hee-hawing on either side. We waited as the leaden footed beasts made their way to their final destiny. As they passed, I heard the bell from the St. Clair Avenue Public School.

"Great place for a school," I said to Will.

"You haven't lived 'til you've written a math test while being serenaded by pigs," Will joked. "Pigs scream- ing as they're being hoisted up by their back legs and pulled through a wall of flames so the hair that wasn't plucked off for brushes is singed off."

I quivered and said, "Goodnight Irene to that."

"No, it's more like Goodbye, Piglet. Goodbye Piglet, Goodbye Piglet. I'll see you by my eggs."

"Will!"

"Red, haven't you read The Jungle yet? You really don't have a clue, do you?" Will teased.

"You mean the book written half a century ago about meat packing in the States? Before government regula- tion? The one you keep telling me to read?"
Will and I repeated variations on his reading sugges- tions for the past three years. He's been telling me what books to buy and read. "The past is the future! Al at the Metropole!" he half garbled, half sung.

The Jane-Bloor bus came barrelling towards us, its driver with time to make. We hopped on at Britannia Av- enue, then off and on again at the Runnymede loop and then rode the Dundas car downtown for the Metropole, dinner and spirits.

METROPOLE SUMMIT NUMBER ONE—RED'S VERSION

Al was already seated in the main room, jotting notes. A draught sipped, he had blown another nickel on a pickled egg, and yet another on a Polish. The legendary Bernie Black readied the small stage for his piano set. I wondered what tune to call for him to play. The Metropole parlour was three quarters full and would be full in half an hour as Bernie was in the house. Four guys at a table near the back scanned the east wall mural, trying to locate the replica of a specific regimental cap badge. Having found it, they walked closer to admire the detail and inspected it for accuracy. Small-towners who, despite the smoke, felt welcomed in the windowless parlour. John, still here I noticed, nodded, turned to the bar and picked up a couple of ryes and a shandy. Will and I sat down across from Al. I pulled my notebook out of my purse in preparation for our first summit on our newest case. Al looked up and smiled.

"You know, I believe time moves slower in the Junction," he said.

"Time doesn't go fast enough for me," I replied. Al dropped his head and looked.

"The Junction's time is past," Will added.

Al and I both looked at him.

Al said, "Now we solved that riddle, whaddya got on our current one?"

John slid our drinks down. "Hey, redhead," he said. John was a likeable kid.

"Hey, JT," I replied.

"No physical signs of violence leading up to or around the ice house," Will drawled.

"Nobody's volunteering anything, 'cept the guys who place bets with Junior's old man sure knew who he was, 'specially if they welched. Constable Daniel Old out of Number Nine is working the case with a downtown detective and they're not working it hard. One guy at the ice house says the cops fired a couple of shots near Ryding or St. Clair last week. If I'm counting my days right, that fits with the Junior showing up in Winnipeg on Thursday of last week. Oh yeah, Junior broke some packinghouse guy's arm for no apparent reason, so Red thinks the union killed him in retaliation."

"Will! You know what I meant!" I slammed my hand down on the red square table.

Al sat up; we slumped down in our chairs. "Let's stick to business here. Let me see if I got this right. This is what we got. Will's buddy from Hagar Avenue calls on behalf of Mrs. O a little less than two weeks after Junior's body was found in a meat car in Winnipeg. We got a load of suspects already: Mr. O and his two other sons were fighting with Junior in a more public way than usual. Preacher Jack's still trying to keep the Mission afloat and seems a bit too familiar with our bookie's family. The good reverend's receptionist, Kat, had a thing going on with Junior. And then there's all the gamblers who couldn't pay up and had direct dealing with Junior. Now, on this latest thing, Ryding and St. Clair are bounded by tracks. The shots are worth a follow up . . . Junior's murder? Not wild about a possible police connection, those are tough to negotiate. We'll put Red on visiting Keele before we head to downtown central.

But, what's this with some guy's broken arm and the union?" Al asked.

"Junior broke this guy Bert's arm over an auto accident. Maybe some of the packing house brothers paid Junior a visit—looking after their own and all—that's what I meant," I glowered at Will, who was watching a young woman by the front door.

"Check out what the union knows too, Red. And Will, go poke around with your usual guys. I think we got ourselves a case," Al concluded.

I started packing my notebook as though we were finished when Al barked,

"Hey! Hold on a minute. Who the hell put an ad in the afternoon edition we took the case? When I got out there this afternoon, Jack, Cappie, hell, even Mr. O knew we were on it."

Will was mum; I followed his lead. Silence blanketed our table despite the hubbub. I looked over at the board in hopes of finding a credible visual distraction and spied the words "fish and chips" scrawled on the blackboard menu. Finally, Will defensively drew himself up, heroic.

"Who the hell knows where they heard it from? Probably Smith shooting his mouth off again. Roy's dumber than he thinks. Or Mrs. O actually talks to her husband. Mrs. O's gang of cronies gossip their way up and down Maria," An irritated Will splayed both arms. Al narrowed his eyes but sat back deciding not to push it. Probable doubt won, even outside the courtroom.

"May we order?" I asked hoping for a merciful end to this summit's tension, the arrival of a hot meal and the uninterrupted pleasure of Bernie's playing. Besides, my stomach needed something other than a sloshed shandy.

"Sure thing Red," Al said. "Let's order. It's been a tough day. I know the stockyards is your least favourite smell. And Will, good work with your neighbourhood connection. You're paying the rent and then some. Hey, we did a lot in a little time today. How about we make it easy for the kitchen given the full house and all order fish and chips?" Good by me, but Will ordered a western on white toast with dill pickles on the side, on a separate plate.

At last, hot chips dosed with malt vinegar and salt. I watched as Bernie Black entertained the house. Audience members called out song titles with the hope Bernie would not know the song. If he didn't know the melody, he bought the next round for the caller's table. Rarely on the hook for a round, Bernie's repertoire was accomplished and fine. He began the set with a flawless rendition of Dear Hearts and Gentle People. Then he pounded out a rocking Rag Mop and slid into a wry version of Alley Cat. I called for a standard song I knew Bernie knew, but wanted to hear him play Everything Happens to Me. Will immediately quipped if once, just once for him, I might call for a Sinatra-like Polka Dots and Moonbeams while Bernie lightly touched the piano keys releasing Everything's opening notes. We stayed until the end of the first set and walked into a cold damp evening along King until turning north.

Canada Life's new beacon flashed tomorrow's weather across the avenue illuminating Osgoode Hall's gated lawns with jolts of colour. The red from the beacon's top undulated with the falling white lights of its tower. Cloudy, but colder tomorrow morning. Al and Will talked about the Don Jail break out and the amount of police resources that must be designated to find the three escaped bank robbers. Past the embassy and office buildings, we turned west along the curve of Dundas and then, a few blocks later, north up Huron.

Will and Al waited on the sidewalk until my key turned in the front door of the Lloyd George Apartments. After we bade each other good night, I lugged myself up a flight of stairs past the dark landing, up another, then left down the hall to my door. I turned the key, stumbling five steps into the room and fell on the bed fully clothed. I slept motionless all through the night.

NOVEMBER 14, 1951
AL AGAIN–AL'S VERSION

I left the West End YMCA early to grab a bit of breakfast at the Venus Lunch and spend a bit of time touching bases with the boys at the Vigor Oil gas station. When I got off the bus, Pappy Kedwell, who with his sons ran the Imperial Oil station across the street from the Venus, nodded and smiled. Inside, Cuzo and Jimmy were working their tails off to accommodate the drovers who were grabbing a quick unauthorized break, having just driven a small herd up the cattle lane from the stockyards. The lane ran parallel to St. Clair Avenue behind the houses on the south side from Dods Avenue to Cobalt Avenue. These were the houses fronted by the Canadian National Railway track that curved north at Cobalt where they joined the CPR tracks right behind Kedwell's station. I grabbed an empty stool at the counter and as soon as I had, Jimmy slipped a plate of scrambled with bacon and white toast and a steaming cup of coffee in front of me.

While I ate, I thought about one of the things that bothered me about this case: as the West was cattle country, there didn't seem any reason to ship beef in a refrigerated boxcar from here to there. Seeing an opportunity, I asked the drover sitting on the next stool. He explained that they raised a lot of beef out west but didn't ship it all the way to Toronto to be slaughtered. They shipped most of it east to Winnipeg, or southeast to Chicago or Omaha. The beef we ate was raised in Eastern Canada and the States. We shipped dressed meat back east, but when the market got out of balance, we would ship dressed beef to Winnipeg, Chicago or Omaha for distribution and consumption. It was a reciprocal arrangement. If dressed beef was in short supply in Eastern Canada, freight car loads would be shipped, usually from Winnipeg,to ease the situation. Question answered.

As I strolled over to the Vigor Oil station, I considered the possibility that the body might have gone out West by something other than one of those three normal routes. An apparently empty boxcar would have been shunted into a packing house, iced, and readied to ship the dressed meat to market. It had been deliberately dispatched to Split-Lip, Saskatchewan or wherever the hell the body had been found by a person or persons so far unknown. I'd have to stick Will with the job of finding and tracing the paperwork. He hated that kind of stuff.

Bobby Walker was draining a few gallons into a big black 1949 Buick Roadmaster—the kind with the round air vents on the side of the engine deck—and smiled as I walked towards him.

"Hi Bobby, is the boss around?"

"Yeah," he said, "he's up in the office. Go on up."

I climbed the stairs to the room that served as an office and emergency sleeping quarters. Eddie was studying a list of names and addresses which I knew from experience was one of the fuel oil customer lists, not a physical record or book where he recorded the odds, bets accepted and the punters' identity.

Vigor Oil had a tank truck that they used to deliver fuel oil. As they were located next to the CPR spur running from the huge Lambton Marshaling Yard to the packing houses, they had a small siding of their own. On that siding would be a railway tank car which carried fuel oil to keep the truck loaded. Periodically, Eddie would phone and order another railway car full of fuel oil. If it arrived too soon, the tank truck driver would have to work overtime to empty the one on their siding and a lot of little customers would get their tanks topped up so they had enough fuel to keep them warm until the snow melted—and we hadn't had a warm day in weeks. When the next tank car arrived, they hauled the empty one away and presumably back to the oil refinery, but I didn't know that for sure. I had taken more of an interest in railway practices since we got involved in this case. Now I wondered if the truck doubled as a mobile betting and collection office.

It struck me that Eddie knew about rail cars and shipping. He could be a big help. He could also be a suspect. The more I thought about it, the more it seemed a possibility. I knew he kept kosher and probably attended and supported the same shul as Mr. O and his family.

"Well?" Micalef said, "I hear that you're doing the Dick Tracy thing and now you've come here to sweat the truth out of me, which is too bad because I am sweating so much over this fuel oil business that I've got nothing left for you."

"Eddie! Dick Tracy is a cop. I am not a cop. My partners and I are investigators."

He didn't say another word. He hadn't moved. I realized that there was someone else in the room, someone Eddie wasn't too fond of. I felt stupid. The big black Buick sitting at the pumps had no driver. This is not the big black Buick end of town. I should have known something was wrong. The only luxury cars that drove into the area belonged to the senior staff of Canada Packers, cars which were fuelled, maintained and everything else in their own staff garage.

I went to turn around when Norbert O's hard voice expelled "Siddown McFuck. Having your ass in a chair is a lot more comfortable than having your face in the floor."

My shoulders stiffened. I knew the voice. Hated that nickname. Knew my hands were balled into fists. Not that Norbert and I didn't get along well enough most of the time. It was just that he had this annoying technique of being abrasive as hell until you were ready to blow a gasket. Then, and only then, he'd turn on the charm and no one did a better job of playing Mr. Nice Guy than Norbert O.

A few years back, I had developed an interest in a really nice girl named Cora. I was too young to be involved in a heavy relationship and she was even younger. Everybody in the neighbourhood knew about the situation. One day,when I was playing nicky-nicky to warn of the approach of the local constabulary while the Maria Street Dark Boys were shooting craps behind the groundskeepers building in Ryding Park, Norbert had come up with this name. It didn't catch on but he invariably used it when it suited his purposes.

"You're an investigator?" he said with more than a hint of sarcasm. "What are you investigating?"

I didn't answer. I could be just as annoying as he could, and right now it suited me. Gaining confidence with the thought, I stood up. I was about half a foot taller than him and my athletic youth had left me with a looseness that made fat-assed people like Nobby wonder whether precipitating a confrontation was a good idea. I didn't wait for an answer.

"Catch you later Eddie," I said as I shouldered my way past Norbert and out the door to the stairway.

"Yeah!" chuckled Eddie. "Come for tea, why don't cha?"

As I walked back across the service station lot, my memory jumped into gear. Bobby was just about to fill another customer's tank. As I passed him, I asked, "Eddie still flying?"

"Oh yeah!" he said, "and the company's still paying."

"Where does he keep his aeroplane?" I said, fishing deeper.

"Orillia, mostly, but sometimes at the Island."

I had gotten more info than I had expected. Not only did he have an aeroplane, but it was equipped with floats. It could be an amphibian but they were unusual. He alone, or with others, could have iced the brother, flown him to some place west of the 'Peg or Chicago or

Omaha and dumped the body in a freight car. Possible, but not likely. We needed more straight info about how he died and all the other things you usually get from the coroner and the police.

I crossed St. Clair Avenue to catch a westbound bus and connect with a Dundas streetcar. While waiting, I thought about what to do next.

I saw Red walking along St. Clair. She did not seem to be enjoying the distinct slaughterhouse stench.

TALKING WITH THE UNION—RED'S VERSION

I left the checking of office messages and mail until later in the afternoon. During a long soak in the claw foot tub, I decided my route to the stockyards: Spadina Avenue to Harbord Street to the St. Clair Avenue car. While the Harbord streetcar would leave me on the wrong side of Keele again, a transfer might provide an opportunity for another chat with Frank the Motorman. As I'd be walking a lot on a cool day, I opted for a pair of black slacks. Every Toronto woman knows, auto exhaust knocks the hell out of your nylons. If you walked or stood close to the road, your nylons would age, gape and run horribly. I threw yesterday's $1.29 in the trash and put on my slacks. To hell with the looks from the old-timers. With my bachelor apartment behind me, the sun broke through the clouds. I took it as an omen.

Up on St. Clair Avenue, I lost my gamble on the route. Not only was the motorman different, the ride was not half as entertaining as yesterday. On the long walk past the plants, I confess that I held my scarf in a discreet way, around my mouth and nose. I felt Will and Al chastising me, even when they were somewhere else. Drivers honked once in a while. Why men thought this action appealed to the honked-at, I will never understand. As I walked, I looked down the gated road towards the ice house. Mr. Lean was not on— a beefier guy was splitting the ice. Other than that, nothing had changed.

After the cattle finished the trudge across St. Clair at Symes, I neared the union office, still smarting from the poke Will gave me about blaming Junior's murder on the Packinghouse Workers and from Al's check-it-out command. As I approached, kids busted out the front and side doors of St. Clair Avenue Public School, jumping and whooping to each other, buoyant upon release for a recess. Games of double dutch and ball hockey erupted with liberated fury. Groups formed here and there, each fed from the boys' and girls' doors on either side of the two-storey building. All the kids breathed enthusiastically, not bothered by the fleshy stench in the air. Beyond the school ground lay the pogey gardens with a man and woman at opposite ends, plots bedded and fences checked. Worth a visit in the evening, I thought, when more gardeners might be out doing the same.

I walked west from the school and a short plump woman with a purple dress and bib apron gingerly swept the walk in front of her steps, a signal she was at the end of her house cleaning. She smiled, said "Hello dear," and toddled back up the wooden stairs to the front porch. The storefronts stood before Britannia Avenue with all of its 24 semi-detached, storey-and-a-half houses. Britannia Avenue is a stockyard dead end with a wood fence physical demarcation between the city of

Toronto and the county of York. Will said the county kids are even tougher than the kids on the city side.

Back at the top of Britannia, the corner storefront was rented by two locals—Canada Packers and Swifts—of the Packinghouse Workers Organizing Committee. If luck was with me, Steve would be in the office. I met Steve in 1948: our paths crossed when we campaigned for Bill Temple. Temperance Bill, as many called him, ran for the Co-operative Commonwealth Federation as a Member of the Provincial Parliament in the riding of High Park. For months, Temple conducted his campaign in his Royal Canadian Air Force uniform. Not only did he look smart, the uniform reduced the number of slammed doors when he went door-to-door canvassing for votes.

More significantly, Temple ran against the sitting Conservative Ontario Premier, George Drew. Temple and the Co-operative Commonwealth Federation won, despite campaigning with funds of only a thousand dollars compared to Drew and the Conservative's fifty thousand. I worked on an organization overseen by Steve—I was an ace both with the stubborn Gestetner of countless letters and pamphlets and with the formidable women's league of door knockers, envelope stuffers and baked goods sellers. I got on with Mary Temple too, when she came by the office. I learned about solidarity and organization. We worked long hours, never minding the donkey work, as we felt a win in our hearts—not only did we have the loquacious Bill Temple, but the neighbourhood was solidly ours as well.

On that cool June eighth night, we listened to the results roll in, subdivision by subdivision, in the crowded

Dundas committee room with the organizing team and, later, a growing crowd of volunteers. Results lagged in from a house or two as the poll captains were known Conservatives who would not let our scrutineers use their house phones. Never mind. The room moved with the pending victory. By the time Bill arrived, we all knew it was ours. We jumped up and down, hugged each other, shouted names as friend after friend arrived at the office. This small town girl finally felt at home in the big city. Dundas was impassable as the polls closed. Supporters arrived in cars with horns blasting and created an impromptu parade snaking down to Keele and back around the neighbourhood again. Bill was hoisted up on a car and the papers were forced to send out photographers to our part of town to cover the victory. Besides the phenomena of Bill Temple beating Drew—a sitting Premier—the CCF became the official opposition. In politics, the first time win is euphoric. The future was ours.

As the night rioted on, Steve and I left the celebrations, snagging a ride in an old Ford with two of Steve's buddies, Andrew and James. Those two were already three sheets to the wind. We headed for the wetter water of Dovercourt, where Eamon Park picked up a seat for the CCF. Eamon was a passionate steelworker and CCF activist with a brogue, warmth and energy. All in all, a winning candidate. Park was not one to back off from calling voter fraud what it was. Despite the voter high jinks, Park held a real victory party and there, Steve introduced me to Al. What Al was doing there, I never quite figured out. I suspected his presence involved a woman. In any event, Al hired me on the spot on Steve's say-so . I quit my part-time secretarial job and started at Al Green's office above Yamada's Photo Studio the following day. He kindly made me an immediate associate. Guess you could say Al Green and Associate looked better on the card. Associates looked better still, when Will officially joined the firm six months later.

Three years after being a campaign worker, I swung open the door to the union storefront, this time as an investigator. Steve was in. His desk faced the front door where he banged away at an adding machine with one hand and paged through a set of invoices with the other. Steve was the son of a founding member of the Packinghouse Workers' union. He helped out his old man, in younger days, by ferrying people down to the basement after they gave the melodic triple knock on their Britannia Avenue back door and later, by helping with hisdoor knocking, books and minutes.

Steve did not give the impression that he heard the jingle of the bell or noticed a presence in the room. I waited until he finished adding what seemed to be a disagreeable set of invoices.

He looked up and started. Smiling, Steve stood, "Dottie! Where ya' been? Jeez, I thought you were Harry coming back from downtown. You open the Corner Pocket yet? Everybody's waiting for you to open that bar that you were always talking about."

"No, not yet," I said. Steve knew me as Dorothy or Dottie before Al nicknamed me Red Ball. We caught up on this and that for a few minutes and he tried to rope me in for some work for the November 22nd provincial election—when I left my first Toronto flat, the High Park CCF riding team lost track of me. I'd moved out of my modest flat on Humberside Avenue to the small apartment on Huron a year ago. I did not miss my intrusive landlords, but I did miss the proximity to the neighbourhood and to St. Cecilia's. No matter.

Finally, I said, "I'm working with Al on a big case. I can't afford the time right now, but might pull the vote for a bit on the 22nd if that helps at all. Sorry I can't do more, but like everybody, I gotta pay my rent. That said, rent aside and all, somehow our provincial campaign seems less spirited than in 1948."

Steve shook his head. "It's tough. We don't have the troops that we had in '48. Expectations for change were high when we won. Now we're the opposition and things aren't as bad as they were then. At least, not as bad as on the surface of things. Twelve Steps to a Better Ontario is a solid blueprint for government and the working class, but doesn't set fire in the neighbourhoods. We should do okay, though. Anyways, can I ask what your big case is?"

"We're investigating Junior O's death," I said bluntly.

Steve let out a long, slow whistle. "That's a tough one, Dots. Junior was a nasty piece of work. Most of the guys, though not the type to speak ill of the dead, aren't too choked up by his demise. It's like Junior had no humanity. He was all brawn, no brain. He'd sooner break your arm than give you a break."

"Speaking of broken arms," I said, "Whadda ya know about Junior's run in with Bert?"

"Oh ho! You have been out and about, haven't you?" said Steve. "But Bert's arm is old news—must be over a year ago now. At the time, it created quite the stir. Bert borrowed a Meteor but driving . . . let's just say driving isn't Bert's strong suit. He cut Junior off turning west off Runnymede onto Dundas. Bert's fault. Junior jumped out of his car, walked over to the driver side and waved Bert out. Bert gets out. Junior belted him and jumped up and down on his arm. Bert is a big guy, but shy. Keeps to himself. He didn't deserve what he got. There was some talk of paying a midnight visit to Junior, but it never went anywhere. Junior's old man saw a problem coming and, like any good business man, bellied up with some cash. A thousand bucks for Bert's family. Packers' gave Bert his job back after a couple of weeks. We made sure he and his kids got food. That was that."

I whistled. "A thousand bucks is a lotta cash."

"Also a lotta smarts," replied Steve. "Mr. O doesn't play footsies with the cops like a lotta the other bookies do. He doesn't have to, Mr. O's too big. Let's just say, Mr. O took a direct route to avoid a complaint that might turn into a visit from the local police."

Nowhere but in the Junction.

"Look Steve, I gotta head over to Number Nine, but is there anything else about Junior? Can I call you sometime, or drop in again?" I handed him our card.

"Sure, sure, drop by anytime. The only other thing you might wanna know is that our man, Temperance Bill, hated the family O's business with a passion, second only to his hatred of the liquor racket. You know Bill voted against allowing sports on Sundays last year. Mr. O was ticked given his past support for Bill, unofficial though it was. Since the Sunday vote, Junior was spotted more than once in the evening, hanging outside Bill and Mary's place. One evening, Mary came out and stood on the front porch staring at Junior 'til he took off. Bill was stomping mad when he heard about it. Why Junior threw kerosene on Temple's fire, I'll never know."

I smiled at the thought of Mary standing tall on her front porch in spite of Junior's bully tactics. "Thanks for letting me in on that one, Steve."

"Anytime, Dots. Drop back soon. Hey, we're counting on you on the 22nd. Wait a minute, why don't I give you a lift?"

BBC–WILL'S VERSION

I took the Carlton tram to Spadina, the tiny Jewish quarter of our whiter-than-white berg. I wasn't a member of that ancient race that I'd come to see though, so I kept my head down as I passed a cigar stand, two delicatessens—corned beef and Kosher dill for a dime—and a haberdasher or three 'til I was standing in front of the new nightclub on the block, El Mocambo. The door was locked, it being too early for patrons, but I could hear the faint thud of a band practising upstairs. Above me, dark but still impressive, was a giant neon palm tree complete with neon coconuts. I heard a break in the music so I hammered on the thick, wooden door. There was little chance that my knocking could be heard upstairs, but I felt foolish just standing there. A couple of orthodox-dressed—probably tailors— gave me a pair of dirty looks as they passed. I gave them the same back just to be fair but it made me feel more foolish. I was relieved to hear the lock unbolt and the door open to reveal my old buddy, Body Bobby Crews.

"Wills!" He smiled with about three dozen teeth.

"BB!" I smiled back at him, squeezing past his enormous frame into the bar. He wasn't nicknamed Body for nothing.

"Getting cold," he said of the actually pretty mild November afternoon.

If you've never been to a nightclub during the day, when it's closed, I mean, you haven't missed much. It can be unsettling, in fact. The ghosts of a million cigarettes and a thousand spilled ales combine in the air for an acrid stew of foul smells, with a sickly sweet base note of cheap perfume.

The door slammed behind us as the band struck up their rehearsal again, a cover of Frankie Laine's Jezebel sounding incomplete without BB's double bass to give it its bottom.

"Sorry to interrupt," I said once we'd reached the tiny dressing room on the third floor.

"Needed a bit of a break," he said, unscrewing the top of a flask, and smiled when he saw the thirsty look looking back at him. He took a pull then passed the flask. I gave it a little kiss myself and passed it back.

"I can give you five minutes," he capped the hooch and pocketed it. "What gives?"

"You hear about Junior?" I said it easy, but I was watching him pretty close.

"Yeah. I heard." He looked okay. Unruffled. Still, I waited for more. I took the makings from my coat. Rolled one while I waited.

"Come on Will, that was a long time ago," his eyes were pleading. "Thought the boy got it out west. My alibi is I was here on Spadina." His eyes were laughing now. I was glad. I always liked BB pretty good.

"You don't need no alibi," I lied, "I was just wondering if you'd heard anything is all."

"Yeah, I heard that cracker finally got his. And I heard, can't remember where, that that made us pretty happy, know what I mean?" BB's eyes were still laughing. Junior and BB went way back. BB liked a flutter on the ponies and I knew that Junior had given him a slap once. BB felt he deserved that slap only because he hadn't slapped Junior right back. At least now I was pretty sure that was the case.

"Sorry Beeb. Had to come ask though, hope you understand."

"Yeah, well, if you're gonna go speak to everyone Junior ever ruckused with, you're gonna have a pretty full plate." He took the smoke from my hand, tried for a pull but it was cold. I lit it for him with my big regimental Zippo.

"Whattya think?" I asked.

He closed his eyes half way, breathed a vast plume of smoke over and around me and said so softly that I had to lean into the smoke to hear better, "Could be you're right thinking it's payback for his being a hot head debt collector for the family business. Could be, as I heard just this morning that it was over some woman . . . or could be biblical in nature. You know, like Cain and Abel." He dropped the smoke to the dressing room floor. I thought he was stepping on it but he stepped over the butt and left the room without another word. I watched the smouldering ash 'til it stopped smoking.

NUMBER NINE—RED'S VERSION
I accepted Steve's offer of a lift to the Toronto police

station, Number Nine on Keele Street, south of Dundas. It was not far, but the thought of cutting across the tracks on my own or losing time walking and riding buses was unappealing. Out the front door, Steve left a note that he would be back in 15 minutes and rattled the door lock. We turned down the length of the storefront on Britannia, right into the narrow lane and left as the L-shaped lane jutted northerly. In faded black paint, across the lane's fence was a scrawl 'Kilroy Was Here.' Above the block words was a line drawing of a round head with an elongated nose, two dash eyes, a few dash hairs and two round hands peering over a wall. Kids or a veteran, who knows. I did know Steve kept his Meteor parked in his old man's wooden garage toward the end of the schoolyard. I waited as he pulled back the door. He backed it out carefully, tightly manoeuvring each way. The Meteor was out. I slammed the garage door shut and jumped in. Once clear, we turned up Britannia Avenue and veered right onto St. Clair Street West.

"My, the Meteor is a peppy car, or is it the Meteor's driver who's peppy?" I remarked after slamming against the passenger door.

Steve laughed, "Yeah, yeah to both."

"Where did you come across these charming green tartan seat covers?"

As we veered onto Runnymede, Steve replied, "My mother offered to make them when I got the car. She bought the fabric on sale at The Dressmakers' Supply Company down on Bay at Bloor. I didn't realize the fabric was green tartan when she offered to sew the covers for me. I don't have the heart not to use them. Besides, what the heck. It saves wear on the seats." Mercifully,

Steve turned on the heat against the morning chill.

As we turned left at Dundas, I looked for Al and Will. They were around here somewhere. Near Pacific, Steve got the better of a streetcar, then waved and honked at a friend. Though the sidewalks on both sides crowded with dozens of shoppers and strollers, I cast a longing look back as we sped past Hunt's Bakery. Once we reached Keele, I thanked Steve for the ride that saved me half an hour in travel time. The clock ticked on cases. He reminded me of the election on the 22nd again and, in turn, I reminded him that my participation pended on being excused by Al and the dictate of the case.

"Yeah, yeah. Case, shmase," he said. He left me on the sidewalk and peeled off in the Meteor faster than necessary. Steve was inspired, no doubt, by the proximity of the station.

Three Fords and a bicycle were parked directly in front of the station. The building was flanked by its garage and the fire hall. The hall was set back from the street while the southern garage jutted out 10 feet beyond the station. The two-and-a-half story building boasted a square tower and white painted stone over and under its rectangular windows. Staunchly Edwardian, the brown brick station was unwelcoming to approach.

Past the front door, a narrow hall led to a squarish room divided by a cured wooden counter. On the other side were desks with police constables either talking on black phones or pounding on Underwood typewriters. Cigarette smoke hazed the view. On this side of the counter, a young boy was renewing his bicycle plate. His skinny frame was as taut as if his spine was being pulled upward by a string. The boy listened as the constable slowly imparted the wisdom of road rules and hand signals. Fifty cents and a signed paper sat on the counter. The boy bobbed his head rapidly when asked if he understood. The constable took the money and the boy took the paper. Warned and renewed, the boy ran out down the hall.

Now, it was my turn.

The constable on desk duty greeted me.

"What can I do for you today, young lady?" he asked while rubbing his hands together. He smiled broadly and leaned forward slightly.

"Hi. Well, I'm looking for Constable Daniel Old," I said.

"Really. A young lady like you? Who may I say is looking?" he replied with his two elbows on the counter.

I offered our card, decided to use my formal name and showed my hand by saying, "Dorothy Brophy with Al Green and Associates. I understand Constable Old's investigating Junior O's murder."

"Whoa, you just said a mouthful," he said to the card. "I'll get him for you."

The constable turned and yelled over to an officer almost out the room, "Get Old out here, will ya? Tell him he's got a lady visitor here on the bookie bad boy business." Five long minutes later, Old appeared through the door from the back.

Old is young. I doubted if he was more than 24. Tall and thin, he had a round face with blue eyes and short blond hair. He strode toward me and ignored a naughty taunt from a fellow officer. His dress and grooming were impeccable: He tied his tie right and cleaned his finger-nails white. I smiled at him and he nodded straight-faced back. Old was a serious young man.

"How may I help you, ma'am?" Old said.

I winced at the word, extended a card and replied, "Dorothy Brophy, Al Green and Associates. I'm one of the associates. We're investigating the death of Junior O and I heard you are too. Is there somewhere we might talk for a minute, compare notes?"

After a long stare, he nodded and walked towards the waist high door separating the public from the police, unlatched the door and swung it open. Old was an officer of few words.

"This way, Miss Brophy," said the constable. Past the rectangular room and the back door, we turned down a narrow hall. At the hall's end, he gestured me toward a small windowless room with four chairs around a blond table. I sat in a chair, making sure I faced the door and Old sat kitty corner, leaving the door open. Officers passed through the hall and up a flight of stairs, joking with each other. A shift change was my guess.

"I have 10 minutes. What would you like to know Miss Brophy?" Old opened the conversation.

"Well, actually, everyone calls me Red. My hair and all. You can, too," I countered, smiling.

Old looked down at the card, raised one side of his mouth and said nothing. He looked back up at me with a straight face. His back was straight too.

Silence, save for the tick of the clock.

"Okay, Constable Old. I get it. I'll go first. Let's start with the facts. We're both investigating a murder. A murder that got coverage in the pages of The Star and Tely. Junior O, the Junction bookie's son, was found shot dead inside a refrigerated freight car in St. Boniface, Winnipeg on November 8, 1951. According to the reports, as the body was discovered on the CPR line, the Royal Canadian Mounted Police were investigating until a Winnipeg coroner concluded the time of death set the murder 20 to 40 hours earlier, probably where the car originated from, Toronto, on November sixth. As the murder took place probably in the vicinity of the stockyards, the RCMP reassigned the case to Toronto Police. Correct?"

"Correct."

"Junior was shot in the stomach."

"Correct."

"Junior had many enemies hereabouts. Gamblers, mainly."

"Correct."

Old kept steady.

"We're agreeing on so many facts already! We'll have this solved in no time," I tried for a smile but failed. "You're very serious, Constable Old."

"Eight minutes, Miss Brophy," he replied.

"Eight minutes, that's it, huh? That's all. Eight minutes. Funny, word on the street—especially on Maria Street—is no official organizations, especially the Toronto Police, are spending time on this case."

"Excuse me?" Old said.

"You heard me. The RCMP kicked the case when they figured the time of death put Junior in Toronto. Took a few days to figure it too. I heard the Toronto Police are going through the motions from a motorman, as well as a Packinghouse worker yesterday. Apart from the standard official comment—what was it, something like—'Toronto Police consider the death suspicious and are currently investigating events leading up to the death,' the only other action from police was a drive around St. Clair to hand out a few cards. Packinghouse workers say you're more concerned with having the case kicked your way than solving it."

"Miss Brophy, did I hear you right? Did you say the Toronto Police Force is not expending the necessary rigour to solve our cases? Are you saying the Toronto Police Force is neglecting their sworn duty to serve and protect? Surely, that's not what you intend to imply about the Toronto Police Force, Miss Brophy." Old leaned across the table towards me.

I achieved exactly what I needed to avoid. Al would brain me. I tilted forward too and said slowly, "Constable Old. That is not what I said. I said that's what Toronto citizens are saying."

"Really. I'd like to take your word on that one, but that's not what we have heard. What, please tell me, is Miss Brophy saying?" Old replied with an equally slow cadence.

I sighed, slumped back and threw my head with the drama of Elizabeth Taylor toward the back of the chair. I replied, "Red. You can call me Red. What I'm saying is the Toronto Police have, at the very least, real obstacles in solving this murder. The fact that Green and Associates were hired to solve it already shows a doubt that Toronto Police will. Given the family business, some citizens suspect doubt is actually a reluctance.

Besides, I know you have your hands full, I read the papers like I said. The Princess coming on a visit to the city requires both crowd control and protection. After the royalty visit, three bank robbers saw their way out of the bars in the Don Jail. The break got more newspaper ink than our man Junior and, I'm willing to bet, more central police resources. The banks and law enforcers need Boyd and the Jacksons back behind those repaired bars. Especially now, the need is even greater as our Toronto citizens are cheering for the bank robbers. And as a Number Nine constable, the call box still flashes on the beat that needs walking. Those bike licenses need renewing. Up and in, it's a busy time at Number Nine.

The problem is, as our motorman said, 'A murder's a murder.' Somebody killed Junior O and we don't know who it is. Listen, Al Green and his two associates are working exclusively on this homicide. Maybe you don't know, but Al and Will grew up around here and I lived on Humberside for a year. We know the folks around here and have a couple of suspects in mind already. Why can't we help each other out and compare notes? Let's get our murderer. That is what Miss Brophy is saying."

Besides a slight shift when I mentioned the Don Jail escape and a raised eyebrow when I mentioned Al and Will were locals, Constable Old stayed steady.

"I believe you are sincere," Old said.

It was my turn for stillness; I had done enough work in this interview. I wondered if he'd share anything.

"I know a murder's a murder. Truth is, the locals either don't trust me or don't take me seriously. My age. My recent arrival. Who knows? Maybe they can tell I'm from Long Branch and such. Won't tell me a thing. I'm working with Detective Sergeant Sullivan from downtown. Also, the number one, two and three priorities are catching Edwin Boyd, Leonard Jackson and Willie Jackson. The Jacksons aren't related, you know.

You have to understand, they come in two or threes, rob banks and threaten managers, tellers and customers, sometimes innocent women and children. They use hand guns, rifles. Screaming at everybody. They are out there somewhere in the city or suburbs, right now. Probably planning another robbery. We're doing a series of raids on west end taverns, intelligence has them in Toronto's west end. This is all off the record, of course." Old held up one hand showing his palm and nodded. I nodded back.

"But back to Junior," I replied.

"But back to Junior O. His mother came here two days ago. All shook up. Yelling about us firing shots last week on Britannia or Victoria or some other place. We were there . . . chasing a hobo out of a yard. Nothing to it. We lost him to York county. But I couldn't make heads or tails of her. Why don't these people understand that screaming louder doesn't help? We try to stay out of there."

Old slipped in more ways than one.

"Outta there?" I said. Again he shifted in his chair.

"North of the tracks. Except when called. Between the dung, the soot and the fumes. God, it stinks," Old confided. "Anyway, about all we got is a dead son, a screaming mother and a dozen happy gamblers. A reporter from The Star keeps calling on it. I don't call back. Detective Brian Sullivan and I are visiting a couple of his gambling finks tomorrow. Wanna add anyone to our list?"

"Nah, not now anyway. How about I get back to you after I meet up with Will and Al tonight? Call tomorrow?"

"Sure. That'd be good." Old stood to leave.

"What a pair we make. See that. We finished in nine minutes," I replied.

Constable Daniel Old finally smiled. "See you 'round, Red."

NIGHT AT THE BALLET—WILL'S VERSION

It was dusk and getting dark as I ran for the College tram at Spadina (not Spadeena, for some reason, in spite of its origin in the old Toronto family of that name. Spadina. Rhymes with wine-a. Though if the Spadinas were anything like the rest of their Orange Family Compact brethren they'd be teetotalers, so it should read: rhymes with whine-a).

I took the car to Yonge and got off at Eaton's College Street. The fancy Eaton's. Made almost impossibly more fancy by tonight's shindig in its seventh floor auditorium. A ballet, can you imagine? Not, they'd have you know, some random one off, but the debut of a national ballet troupe. Sleepy backwater Toronto playing host (did I mention it was at Eaton's Department Store?) to the brand spanking new National Ballet Company. Should be good for a laugh, so I'd been planning to poke my head in for a while. If I'd needed a better reason than that to attend, something told me it might be a chance to see my erstwhile employer in her natural habitat.

I mean Mrs. O of course. I'd read somewhere that she'd persuaded her old man to kick some of the old ill-gotten in to be one of the sponsors of the venture. The National was that new and underfunded that they weren't looking too carefully in any of the mouths of the gift horses trotting their way. If I got close enough to the old dear, I knew I'd find a way to have a quick word with her. Despite Roy warning me off, it felt strange working for someone I was forbidden to contact. Forbid me and I'm like a dog who wants a bone.

I was on my own as I'd been unable to persuade any of my friends in going to a ballet—truth be told, they really weren't that type of crowd.

The foyer at Eaton's College was packed, a hundred people at least waiting for elevators to the seventh floor and the auditorium. Waiting, I remembered how Toronto's first elevator was in the Timothy E's flagship store. It was before my time, but the story goes that you could only take the lift up, stairs and gravity would see you down. Thinking of the poor shopper loaded with parcels, blindly stumbling down, cursing that policy made me chuckle out loud and a few overdressed ballet fans moved a step away from me. I smiled at a trio of older ladies—blue rinse brigade all the way— my chuckle almost strangled itself as I recognized one of them.

"Sorry ladies!" I tipped my hat towards them, "I'm just that pleased that we finally have a first class ballet in this country!"

I moved closer to them with my hand outstretched. "What a pleasure to see you here, Mrs. O."

That stopped her. She raised an eyebrow and tried to place me, I could practically see the gears and levers move as she came up short.

"I'm sure I've not had the pleasure," she ventured, moving a step behind her cronies.

"Will Jones, mum," I extended a hand. She had to step out from behind her friend to take it. She had no choice, she was raised like that.

I took the old dear's hand. It was dry, felt like straw

wrapped in spiderwebs. I didn't squeeze too hard.

She was still looking quizzically at me so I told her, "I'm from out your way ma'am, the Junction I mean. We have a mutual friend, Roy Smith? He called about your son?"

At the mention of the dear departed, the lights went out in her eyes. Tears welled up and I knew I had played it wrong. One of her pals led her away shooting me daggers while the other blocked my way. "Jones and Smith? Really?"

I got in the queue for a different elevator.

I left the dance, still chuckling at the lengths some will go, yet having to doff my hat (though I don't wear one) to intentions noble, however misguided. I hailed a cab as I'd had my fill of that clattering College streetcar. Seven minutes and one dollar later, we'd pulled up at my Markham Street single. Charles, the cat that I lived with then, was waiting for a free meal. I gave it to him and then made myself a bowl of oatmeal while cutting a couple of grapefruit halves over a chop left over from yesterday. I washed it down with that morning's spare coffee warmed on a gas jest. I ate my ad hoc repast standing, looking out over the fire escape at two-alley toms studiously avoiding each other in the neighbor's backyard. I could hear my upstairs neighbour's radio. It was playing the song BB's band was rehearsing that afternoon at El Mocambo, Jezebel. Over the years I musta heard Frankie Laine sing four or maybe even five versions of that one. But the version that was a hit in the fall of '51 was by far the scariest of them. I was singing along to it, we were getting to the "Jezebel, it was you" part when the door bell rang. I froze. Frankie went on singing from the upstairs radio and I had a moment of panic 'til I remembered that at midnight, it probably wasn't the landlord. Well, hopefully not.

Imagine my surprise when it was Mrs. O.

"Ma'am!" I sputtered. Hell, I practically curtsied I was so shocked.

"Young Will, I'm sorry. I find that we were never properly introduced. I do hope that I've given no offence by arriving so late, I was struck by what you said back at the hall. You must know . . ."

"Of course, please come in," I said making a waving motion with my hand. When I looked up, I found that, like an automaton, I had made my way to the drinks sideboard. Poured a rye for myself since I was there anyway and asked the old dear if she'd join me for one.

"Oh, please," she surprised me, then answered my raised eyebrow with, "Somehow I find I'm not shy around you, my young friend . . . make a rather large measure if you don't mind."

She bent down and gave Charles a quick pat as I poured her a rather large measure.

"I was sorry to hear about Junior," I passed her the drink, then took a good pull on mine. "I knew him, you know."

"What did you mean back there at the hall, when you said I knew of a connection between yourself and my son's recent, ahhh . . . demise, I suppose it was." She looked right through me. She wasn't lying, she didn't know.

"I'm sorry that I approached you, ma'am, under the circumstance. Someone hired me to look at your son's . . . what'd you call it? Demise. Well, hired me and my

58

two associates. Hired us acting, he said, on yer behalf. As your agents, I guess. He was lying though, wasn't he, Mrs. O?" That took the legs out from under her a bit. I helped her to a chair.

"What I was hoping you might be able to help me with," I steamrolled right over her question, "is who exactly stands to gain by Junior's untimely passing? You wouldn't happen to know who his beneficiaries are, would you Mum?"

"I'm not sure. The will hasn't been read yet, though I've known for some time there is a will. I'm executor of the estate, well, co-executor. The will is to be opened and read tomorrow, but again, who hired you on my—"

"Co-executor with who?" I watched her carefully.

"There's three of us. The other two are friends-were friends-of my son. One's a woman I've only ever heard referred to as 'Kat.' The other's a Mission preacher. His name is Preacher Jack."

"Really?" I didn't even try to hide my surprise.

"Yes." She was rooting through her hand bag and came up with a tooled leather cheque book. "Well, Will," she said a little tipsily. I noticed she'd finished her rather large measure of rye. "Well, Will," she said again, "Since you're reluctant to confide in me the name of your client, let's try it this way. I would like to engage your services myself. Perhaps some filthy lucre will loosen your tongue," she giggled at that and wrote my partners and I a cheque.

ONCE MORE–AL'S VERSION

I got off the streetcar when it turned onto the part of

Runnymede Road right in front of the long store. After walking the short sprint to Maria Street, I turned east. When I reached the bakery, the smell of baking bread gave my appetite a boost. As a boy, my mother would send me for an eight-cent loaf that now would cost you 18 cents. Those eight cents were two cents less than the price you would pay at a store or from one of the several bread wagons that circled the district six days a week. Whenever I came through the door, the big burly baker would automatically ask "with seeds or not seeds?" and following instructions, I'd respond with "not seeds" and hand him the eight cents. The bread wasn't wrapped of course, so I stuffed it into the brown paper bag that I had been given along with the eight cents.

The street was unusually quiet. I had forgotten that people worked and thought I'd better get my ass in gear or I'd end up having to find a new job myself.

As I approached the corner of Gilmour Avenue, I noticed Chaim standing out in front of the junkyard he owned and ran. When I was old enough to own a wagon, I would collect junk, mostly scrap paper and and scrap metal.I'd haul it down here(as did others in the district) where this gruff, old bugger would give me a few coins for whatever I had. I felt at the time that I was being taken advantage of but knew I was getting more than I would from the aggy bones man. In later years, I came to realize that Chaim was encouraging our youthful industry by giving us those few coins, which totalled far more than what our junk was worth. He was in fact, a very kind old man.

He motioned me over to where he was standing and before I could say hello he said, "You look for Cap man, yes?"

"Yeah!" I replied, "How did you know that?"

"He say you come around yesterday, you find him at Freeman's Pool Hall. If you come around today he meet you at Alps Restaurant. He have lunch around noon."

My stomach let me know, without checking my watch, that it was almost 12 o'clock and I could leg it to the Alps in a few minutes.

"Thanks Chaim," I said, "Nice of you to take the trouble to let me know."

"No trouble," he said, "Preacher Jack nice man, good for neighbourhood. Everybody say he talk in his church about we not need these kind of peoples around and we feel same. Maybe you collect bad man, bring him to Chaim like scrap for crusher."

He had a crooked smile on his face and I had little doubt about what would happen if he got his great strong hands on the murderer.

"We must talk soon," I said as I turned to go. "I think there are a lot of things you could tell me that would help our side." He chuckled at the last bit.

I set off at a good pace to make sure I caught Cappie at the Alps. I would rather have gotten together with him yesterday as I hadn't enjoyed a game of snooker for a long time.

Freeman's was the larger of the two pool halls in the Junction. It occupied a big area upstairs above the Bank of Toronto at the northeast corner of Keele and Dundas. A block and a half away, on the south side of Dundas Street between Mavety Street and Medland Avenue, the Junction Billiards occupied a storefront area about half the size of Freeman's. Both were invariably busy.

When I was younger and living at home, I preferred the Junction Billiards as did my friends of my youth, Peter, Dan and Cliff. This thought sent me on a detour, a detour to catch Peter. I took ashort distance up Pacific Avenue to Vine Street and then walked along the north side, past Dr. Jackson's Roman Meal Bakery to Irvine's lumber yard . Peterowed me a double sawbuck and I didn't have the bread to cover the cost of lunch. At his request, I had paid his father's tab with the bookie at Vigor Oil. I was not supposed to know that his old man bet the horses.

His brother Harley told me he was at the back of the yard unloading a boxcar of four-by-twos which was a responsibility he had inherited when he was a lot younger and quite nimble. He was able to squeeze into a loaded car and begin the unloading by manipulating the lumber which had been slid into place until there was virtually no space available in the doorway. When I told him what I wanted, he quickly handed me two fins saying that was all he had at the moment and that he would give me the rest when we met at the Saturday poker game. I didn't bother to explain that I probably wouldn't make the poker game as what he had given me would be enough to cover lunch, but I thanked him. A thought popped into my head as I was about to leave.

"Pete," I asked, "What's the difference between a boxcar and a refrigerated freight car?"

"Well," he said, looking a little surprised, "Most of the refrigerated cars have ice compartments at both ends. They're accessed from hatches on the top in opposite corners and charged with ice immediately before the loading and shipping of perishables. You don't remember those things?" he asked. "We used to play tag on the string of cars sitting on the siding on the other side of the pogey gardens when we were kids."

"I never paid much attention to them," I replied smiling, "except to be careful that I didn't step into an open one."

He chuckled as I left. I thought of my partners and their journey to the ice house which had to be closer to the beginning of things than anything else.

I continued down the street, turning south when I got to Keele Street. At Dundas Street, I slipped into the United Cigar Store on the corner and picked up a couple of stogies which we could enjoy after lunch. Exiting, I stood on that corner for a couple of minutes looking south toward the local cop shop, amazed at the Toronto Police Department's unexplained involvement in what increasingly appeared to be a local murder of a local boy. Red would be paying them a visit in the very near future. I didn't envy them.

The Alps Restaurant was on the north side of Dundas, almost across the road from Red's favourite bakery. The bakery had an extensive menu as most did but portions were smaller and prices larger. It was more of a woman's place and I felt a lot more comfortable at the Double R several blocks west.

At the Alps, Cappie was sitting at a table near the back. He was sipping what appeared to be iced tea. The difference between small profit and big profit in the restaurant business was determined, in part, by how fast you could move the patrons out and seat new ones. The other part was how much you could make from the leftovers. Cappie's iced tea was likely the doctored remains of some lady's pot full—par for the course.

"Take a load off your feet Raschi," he said with his usual joviality. "I haven't ordered yet. Just enjoying the local rotgut to sharpen my appetite." Then, addressing the waitress behind me, he ordered, "I'll have a toasted egg salad sandwich and this gentleman will have . . . " he paused, looking at me with raised eyebrows.

"A ham on brown with a touch of hot mustard," I said.

She smiled and asked if I wanted something to drink. I ordered a glass of milk which brought a bigger-than-usual smile to Cappie's face. As he took a belt of iced tea he reached over, plucked a cigar out of my pocket, smiled even bigger, and said, "My favourite kind: unsmoked," which made me smile.

"So, you got something for me?" I asked.

He frowned. "Why don't cha relax and enjoy your food? The kid's dead, right? He ain't going nowhere, right? You don't know who did it, right? Don't hustle your ass to catch somebody when you don't even know who you're looking for."

The waitress arrived with our sandwiches, effectively ending the lecture. Cappie grinned at me.

"You get under my skin Raschi, ya know that? People don't get under Cappie's skin, ya know that?" He chuckled. "You got a rare talent, ya know that?"

"Shut up and eat!" I said, and we both broke into laughter.

Once he finished his sandwich, he lit his cigar and leaned back. "Nakev picked up some information that may be of use to you guys," he said in a very matter of fact way.

This announcement was followed by a lengthy silence. Nakev was one of the Maria Street Dark Boys and it is unusual for one of them to rat another out. Finally, I said "So?"

He took another drag on his cigar and said, "Ya know the dearly departed was chasing the Kat right?"

"Right."

"He was spending a lot of money on her. A lot of money. You know the family we're talking about? They're up to their collective asses in green but Junior's spending more than his share on her."

"Where'd he get it?"

"You tell me smart ass! You're the big investigator," he said.

Then I asked the obvious question: "How, where and when did Nakev come by this information? He's not the family accountant or anything like that is he?"

"No, but his new girlfriend is," he said with a smirk.

"OK. Who is his new girlfriend?" I asked, walking right into it.

"Kat! You stupid asshole. Kat!" and I could hear that tune in the background again . . . There were drifters and commuters. Con men and crapshooters.

Now I had to talk to Kat and Nakev to get an answer to the obvious question: Where was Junior getting the money from? Having come to this momentous conclusion, I checked my watch and headed for Bloor Street to catch the King Street tripper to York Street and confer with my associates over suitable suds.

METROPOLE SUMMIT NUMBER TWO–WILL'S VERSION

I was running a wee bit late for my meeting with Red

and Green, what else is new? They were both kind of glowering at me as I trotted the last few lengths towards them at the good ol' Metropole (we serve no pickled food before it's time).

"Look who the cat dragged in," said Red, a bit disgustedly.

Al looked me up and down with the exaggeratedly patient expression that I swear he saves just for me, before sighing theatrically and looking I guess, towards heaven for the strength to carry on. I caught the barkeep's eye and signaled for a drink while sliding into the chair beside Red.

"Sorry I'm late, ma'am."

She loves it when I call her that. She picked up where she had left off, telling Al about her rendezvous with the cop, Danny Old. As usual, she had done a thorough job and then reported back to us, giving us a succinct and relevant overview of the situation. In spite of that, for some reason I had to get a little dig in.

"So you told him everything you know and got zero in return, as usual?" I asked after yawning somewhat. What can I say? I just love to wind that gal up some.

Her eyes flashed as she ignored me and Al. Al, peacemaker that he is, diffused things with his take on the matter.

"So, Constable Old might welcome our input as we're Junction-born and cooperate accordingly, you think?" He had, as usual, got to the heart of the matter pretty effortlessly.

"Exactly," she was beaming. "I'm going to call him first thing tomorrow."

I winked at her so there would be no hard feelings

over having called her ma'am. Her demeanor softened. She couldn't really hold a grudge, she just wasn't wired that way. I brought the two of them up to date by telling them about my talk with Mrs. O, but not about Roy just yet.

"So you got nothing either, really. We knew there were family tensions," Red tried but her heart wasn't in it.

"One more thing Al," I finished my rye and turned towards him. "I was remembering a bit on my way here that you and Junior have—well, had—a mutual acquaintance . . ."

They were both all ears.

"One I think you should maybe look up."

He started to say something but I didn't let him interrupt.

"Woman you know. Name is Kat."

NOVEMBER 15, 1951
LUCKY STRIKE—AL'S VERSION

After dragging myself out of bed the next morning, I headed to the YMCA for a workout in the gym and a swim before breakfast. The facilities at the West End Y are first-class, well-constructed and maintained. The pristine pool was cooler than I liked it to be but my old body adjusted quite quickly. I shaved in the shower room, dressed and headed west for the Double R and breakfast. I missed the telephone message that had been left with the night clerk.

The regular breakfast traffic had gone to work by the time I arrived. The only person in the place besides the proprietor was Kat and I could tell she was steaming mad at something or somebody. It couldn't have been me, I hadn't done anything. Her being here saved me a lot of walking and helped keep things quiet. I sat down opposite from her in the back booth and her brown eyes looked through me.

"You really are a dink, ya know that?" she shot at me.

"What did I do?"

"You were supposed to be here early. I left a message for you when I called about eight last night and you were out. I'm already late for work and the old man doesn't like it when I'm late." Having spit that out she seemed to mellow a bit.

"I obviously didn't get the message," I confessed.

"What you people need at that place is a female clerk who would make things work properly."

That would really work out, I thought. All kinds of men and boys. All ages, shapes and sizes in various states of undress. They'd be six deep at the counter just wanting to make a little small talk. I let it pass.

"So what was the message?" I asked, in my best blundering style.

"You were supposed to meet me at Fran's at 9 last night so I could tell you I didn't want to be seen with you in the Junction."

"Your new boyfriend jealous?" I reasoned.

"Let us get that straight. I am not anyone's girlfriend. Not Junior's, not Nakev's and not yours."

"I didn't think I was a player in that game anyway," I said, surprised.

She got up to leave, picked up the check which had been lying on the table since I arrived, tucked her purse under her arm and said, "Call me at home after work."

"Where's home?" I asked.

"I live with my mother, idiot."

I was sorry I asked, but I slid around on my seat and watched her sway down the length of the joint to where George waited at the cash register. She was tall and slim—obviously exercising and watching her diet. I liked what I saw. Any healthy male interested in sex would have.

As Kat restored her belongings to her purse George walked toward me to take my order. "The lady paid for your breakfast," he smiled.

By the time I looked, she was gone. I wolfed down a couple of poached eggs on toast and silently debated the merits of having a third cup of coffee when George plonked down across from me with a cup of his own in one hand and the coffee pot in the other. As he warmed mine up I asked him, "What's got up her nose?" I figured he saw and heard more than any of my usual sources.

"I don't profess to understand women," he began. "She's acting like the wife of a very lazy husband."

"George," I said, "I haven't been a player for a number of years now, haven't seen anyone or talked to anyone for a long, long time. Except for dropping in here for coffee once in a while, I've been a stranger to the Junction."

"Yeah!" he said, "It goes to prove it, doesn't it?"

"Goes to prove what?" I was getting quite serious.

"Absence makes the heart grow fonder!" he said laughingly.

"Bullshit!" I said, thinking that with Kat's attitude she was looking more and more like a likely suspect. She certainly had the balls, so to speak. Before leaving, I asked George where he figured I might find Nakev.

"He usually hangs out at the bowling alley," he said, not offering specifically which bowling alley, but there were only two in the Junction and they weren't too far apart. They were several blocks east of where I was, on

the other side of Keele Street in fact, and I debated taking the TTC but finally decided I needed the exercise.
I crossed to the north side of the street so I could have
a look through the front windows of Mr. O's offices,
and as I passed Jaffine's Feed Store, Bernie was leaning
against the front door jamb catching some of the warm
rays of the sun.

"The old man don't like guys following his girl into the
office," he said.

"I appreciate your interest in my well-being, old
friend," I lied. "You have a previous problem with him
because of that?"

"Naw," he lied in turn, "just didn't want an old friend
having a problem that might be avoided."

"Thanks," I said as I walked away.

On my way along Dundas Street, I stopped in at the
West Toronto Music Store to say hello. The owner, Mr.
Lott, was leaving as I arrived and he smiled warmly.
Even though I knew he didn't know who the hell I was,
business owners warmed to people, particularly those
they regarded as potential customers. This was one thing
that I realized was starting to disappear, as the next
generation of business owners were full of themselves
with a "look at me, I am somebody, I own this business,
you are lucky I let you in the door" attitude.

Hughie was smoking one of his own rolled cigarettes,
staring into space, entranced by some piece of music
playing softly over the store's speaker system. When he
woke to the presence of another being, he chuckled and
asked if I were there on his business or my business.

"My business," I said.

"I didn't know the young man. I don't know the

old man. And I don't know the young lady. Six months ago the preacher came in and asked for a recording of a tango. He has been back several times since, maybe as much as twice a month, and invariably buys a tango, I don't know why. I don't know whether he can dance let alone do the tango and I don't care. That's it."

I couldn't resist the opportunity. "How does the young lady figure into all this?" I said using my meanest private eye inflection.

"Well," he said, somewhat taken aback, "The word on the street is she has a bodyguard with a gun who will blow away anyone who gives her a hard time. People suspect that he eliminated Mr. O's youngest who was giving her a hard time."

"You're lying," I said, my mind drifting to the firm's Ivor Johnson .32 revolver. I assumed it was snugly stored in its usual resting place.

"Yes," he said rather nervously. "I don't know anything about her but didn't like to say it. I wasn't lying about the preacher and the tango records though, well, tango or samba or mambo. Latin music, it's all the same to me."

I gave him one of our business cards with the admonition that he was to call one of us at any time if he saw or heard anything that might be important to the case. As I intoned this admonition, I felt I should continue with the usual detective thing, leaving no line of questions unasked.

Instead I left. I wanted to get to the bowling alley and talk with Nakev, but even more than that, I wanted Kat to explain how I became involved with a young lady I had not seen for several years and never dated.

I wouldn't say I hadn't asked her out when we were younger—she had politely refused, explaining she had a previous engagement—so I couldn't figure out what all this "meet me at Fran's at 9 o'clock" or "the Double R at the crack of dawn" business was about.

Moving briskly, I crossed Keele Street going east along the south side of Dundas Street and quickly arrived at the Roseland Bowling Alleys. A large establishment housed about 14 lanes across the ground floor. The Roseland was clean, neat and empty. I approached the snack bar where the owner cleaned the big mirror over the back bar. He seemed to know instinctively that I wasn't going to buy anything and didn't bother to turn around. He could see me quite well in the mirror and I could see him.

"Nakev been in today?" I asked.

"No sir," he said politely. "I kicked his ass out of here a few months back and he hasn't been back since. He was bowling sweeps with a group of honkies who couldn't read or write. The only one keeping score was Nakev who made some serious mistakes with the arithmetic to ensure he won most of the time. Since then, he's been hanging out up the street."

I thanked him and headed for the door.

Though the Lucky Strike Alleys were a little further east, it took me less than five minutes to walk in the front doors. It had 18 lanes all together, six on each of the building's three floors. A little grungy by comparison, but whereas Roseland was empty, numerous groups bowled on Lucky Strike's first floor alleys. I caught up to Nakev on the second floor. Except for the kid setting the pins, Nakev was alone practising. He hadn't changed.

Medium build and still a good looking guy with blue eyes. As I approached, he turned and said, "I know you want to talk. Why don't we bowl a few lines to make us look normal?"

I agreed, and turned to the shoe rental counter. The boy setting pins came down from the end of the alley and asked me what size I wanted. I changed into the size nines, gave him a buck and my black oxfords. He gave me a dog-eared coat-check ticket in exchange. As I turned toward the alley, I caught sight of Nakev's back as he sprinted out the door and down the stairs to the street. It wasn't my day. Nothing had gone right. Then I thought of the stupidity of his actions and the old expression, "you can run but you can't hide," and the same old melody seemed to be broadcasted over the sound system in my head. I thought about it for a minute and asked myself, what has Ace In The Hole got to do with this?

I realized it was getting late so I changed into my oxfords and used the phone book hanging under the pay phone on the wall to look up the Mission's phone number. I checked for Kat's home number too. She wasn't listed but her mother was and I dropped a dime into the phone. I was still getting accustomed to the increase in the tariff from a nickel to a dime. Kat answered on the first ring.

"Look," she said immediately, "I'm sorry to keep changing things but I don't want to upset anyone important. Meet me at Fran's tonight at 9 o'clock and I'll explain the things."

In an offhand way, I had just been told I wasn't important. "Will Nakev be there?"

"No!" She said rather sternly. "I don't date him, except once or twice a couple of years ago. I haven't. And I don't now.

"OK," I said. "Fran's at 9 o'clock." And I hung up.

I was about to leave when the door opened and Nakev came in, head down, walking slowly. He was closely followed by the athletic looking younger rep. and a grim faced Cappie.

"You boys have a nice chat. My boy and I will wait downstairs," said Cappie.

"You should stay," I said. "It would keep things honest, I think."

"Might be interesting too." His face broadened with his usual smile.

Turning to Nakev I announced, "We are not going to bowl a few lines. We are going to have a friendly chat during which you will spill your guts about your business with Junior O." That song was back in my head again. Only now, I heard the melody louder.

STAKE OUT AT THE OLD CORRAL–RED'S VERSION

Mr. Bowes banged the rear door of the cab shut and plopped in the driver seat. He slammed the front door, popped the gear to first and asked what a sweet cookie like me was doing heading up to the Junction before dawn.

"It's a mystery," I replied.

"Ha! Smart one are ya? Ease up. Really, why? Why you heading there so early? Even up in that living hell, a teach don't teach at six in the morning," the cabbie noted as he swung wide onto College Street.

"I'm not a teacher."

"Hmm. Dressed like you are, I venture you ain't a packer either."

"Bingo on that one."

"Come on. Give a working stiff a break. Just wondering. Kinda rough up there, ya know."

Why does anybody meddle in everyone's business? Some days the art of the nonchalant investigation seemed more practised here than in the village of Tweed. I momentarily contemplated telling him the truth—I was on stake out detail in the northwest Junction for Al Green and Associates' detective firm—but decided it was best not to. The cabbie might know somebody who knew someone who knew the staked-out. I may be burnt on a stake out, but never due to my own admission.

Quickly fabricating a falsehood, I said, "Neighbourhood's not so rough if you grew up there like I did. But since you asked, out of concern for my safety and all, I'm babysitting my neighbour's two kids. Her old man is on the morning shift and she's taking care of some errands downtown. She wants me there for tea before she leaves and her kids wake up. As I said on the telephone yesterday, just drop me in front of St. Clair Public School. I'll walk from there. She doesn't need the entire block talking about a big cab hogging the street and letting me out and all."

I leaned back hard in my seat to end the conversation. With all four windows closed, the heater blew hot air criss-cross around the Ford's bountiful back seat, a beautiful sensation on a cold morning. A sensation I might have missed if Al had his way. When he gave me the stake out detail, Al suggested I walk down to the level crossing at Strachan Avenue south of King

Street West, grab the back ladder of a train and ride it up to the Junction like the guys do. But, much to Will's delight, I said I did not think I could. While confident in my physical ability, I was reluctant about breaking the social convention: that feat would be more daring than entering through the men's entrance. Besides, the inevitable soot would signal a first time freight hopper. Even more, I read in the papers judges were fining folks two dollars for trespassing along the CPR line. Of course, the Toronto Commission's buses and cars were still corralled in the barns. Convenience, cleanliness and closure were the reasons I enjoyed the rare pleasure of a cab along Toronto's deserted streets. Heck, every now and then, Will would grab a cab for three blocks and try submitting a crumbled receipt as a business claim. Driving along Harbord Street, the city seemed pleasantly void of commotion save for the odd automobile, alley cat and cheerless smoker. All seemed lost.

The cab turned sharp at Harbord Street's dead end at Ossington, raced past three blocks of comfortable homes on Hepbourne Avenue, then turned briskly at the church and sped along Dovercourt Road, but slowed further north past the semi-detached houses at Hamilton Gear and the rail subway. The two blocks to the north were one of Toronto's best speed trap locations. Bowes heeded the necessity for caution but pressed hard on the pedal as we passed Regal Road School up the hill at Dufferin Street. Simply by turning a corner, you can quickly find yourself in an entirely different neighbourhood.

Nearing Lansdowne, I swallowed my first breath of the wretched abattoir's loathed smell. The northwest Junction's odour walloped the consciousness out of a person's sense of smell and assaulted the tongue and the taste buds at the back of your mouth. Blocked nostrils and open mouth breathing helped minimally. Everybody hated the odour. While Will took a philosophical approach explaining its pungency is truly the smell of fear and death, Al took the storyteller's approach. He scoffed at outsiders like me who talk about one odour, a wretched abattoir odour, when talking about neighbouring receptacles of the plants. Al unspeakably thought, 'what-a-prig'. Well, he thought 'what-a-prig' on his kindest day.

Al described the smells of his former neighbourhood in their specific and separate components. Inside the three square miles where he once lived was the City of Toronto Garbage Incinerator, a City of Toronto Sewage Treatment Plant; four abattoirs with cattle, horse, pig and sheep pens, manure platforms; the Lambton Yards with coal and steam powered locomotives; and numerous trucks hauling in animals and then hauling meat out. More often than not, when Al talked about the Junction—frequently at the Metropole Hotel after a pint or two and admitting he grew up next door to the plants—he began with the pleasant smells in a bid to confuse his listeners. He is a Junction boy after all. Al's old man still worked at Canada Packers, currently in the smoked meat room. Al said the warm room contains delicious scents of salt, sugar, spices, brine and curing hung meat. In the accompanying six-storey smoke house, hook hung hams and bacon and sausage were smoked by a pile of smouldering mound of sawdust on the ground floor. Smoke, spices, cured meat and slow burning wood form one set of smells. Another was his mother's roasts surrounded by floating aromas of a simmering gravy, beef, carrots and cakes escaping through the crevices of his parent's little house out to Britannia Avenue before Sunday dinners. Another set of smells Al remembered was the smell of Ryding Park, the smoke of the winter bonfire mixed with the smell of ice shards and the worn boards after twenty kids got at it with their skates and sticks, pucks chased.

Suddenly, he would shake his head, laugh and wonder aloud how everybody survived the magnificent stink on a daily basis. He started in with the jokes. The smell was not a monolithic singular as us prissy outsiders believed. Everything depended on the winds. When the wind was wrong, the combined smell of a back up at the City's sewage plant off Rockcliffe Boulevard and a pile of dumped garbage awaiting incineration at the City Incinerator on Symes Road as well as the actual process of incineration caused even the most seasoned neighbour to stagger a little upon leaving their homes. When the wind blew from another wrong way, the soot from the rail yards south of St. Clair from Runnymede to Keele dropped a dark patina of dust over everything—laundry, autos, clothes, window and gardens—and lent another subtler dusty odour and taste. Of course, with the final wrong direction, the smells were different again from the four meat packing plants and Ontario stockyard pens. Smells from frightened animals, piles of their manure in the pens and platforms, burning fur or hair or whiskers before and after slaughter, resultant buckets of spilt blood and production of fertilizer from the rest not resulting in meat. One never forgot the acrid smell caused by rendering or boiling of animal parts. And the production at the abattoir production was relentless, 24 hours daily. Finally, when humid and windless and cloudy, all smells conspired with the others in the commitment of crimes against all the living, humans and beasts alike. Al has been known to go quiet at this part in the story.

But now I sat in Bowe's cab with my hankie over my mouth and nose, discreetly I hoped. I dropped the lacy thing back inside my purse when I imagined a glance between Al and Will. We seemed as sailing under the subway over St. Clair Avenue West, almost at Keele Street as the wind blew from the east. In the early dawn, I left a lonesome Huron for the frenetic St. Clair. A navy blue truck with white lettering, C. Symthe for Sand, sped past us, coming from the sand and gravel yard from ways down the hill. At the intersection by Keele Street, a group of workers stood talking by the first of the soiled brown brick buildings that were Swift's. Sardonically, a bold red script was square both on its wall and inside the bill board sign: Bringing Home the Bacon! Swift's Premium. Over on the south side of the intersection, an old Ford pick up truck with a couple of nervous heifers pulled into the small parking lot in front of the Ontario Stockyards building. Another farmer lost in commerce.

Bowes gunned the Ford when the light turned green but cursed when he saw the cattle crossing, some hundred yards past Keele. The small herd was shepherded across St. Clair from the white covered cattle pens over to Swift's. The drovers whacked their canes and called sharply "Hey! Hey! Haw! Haw!" while the cattle lowed and a few bellowed. Their hoofs clacked out of time against the road bed. At the same moment, down a 100 yards off Dods Avenue, cattle cars moved along the rails on the south side of St. Clair to behind Canada Packers. Men walked along the road in pairs, groups or single file at a shift change. "Hello, bro." "Morning brother, milder today." "Yeah, bro . . ." were spoken in all accents and brogues. But then, for a long minute, the squeal of the train wheels against tracks trumped the chorus of cows, men, machinery and trucks.

Suddenly, Bowes snapped with complaint, "It ain't right. I heard that the city is getting rid of this damn cattle crossing and the one past Symes Road. How am I supposed to get people to where they are going? Streets are for automobiles, not livestock! We're in the city, right? Not Thistletown, damn it. Oh, shit. Pardon my French."

"You cursed, you didn't speak another language, right?" I replied.

Bowes looked strangely back at me using the wide rear view mirror.

"Forget it. Sorry. Anyway, just in the name of curiosity, how'd you suggest getting the cows and pigs and sheep from the Livestock Exchange and the 30 odd pens on the south side of the street over to the four plants on the north side without walking them across the street?" I asked.

"That's their problem, not mine. Build a bridge. Dig a tunnel. Drive them over for all I care. Cows shouldn't be blocking the street. Phew. I just want to get away from the stench. Somebody should do something about these cows clopping around, that's all I'm saying."

Bowes scratched his neck and shifted in his seat. The cattle were almost across the street and silently I prayed to St. Christopher that nothing else would cross over to Canada Packers. We were delayed by a truck swinging out of the Packers' loading dock, but Bowes said nothing. Thankfully, the train crossed the street and pulled by the plant. Like Bowes said, at this point I just wanted to get where I was going. Past the pens, loading docks, plants—including the building Al pointed out was once owned by a small packer, Frank Hunnisett, before Canada Packers bought them out—and past the six refinery tanks and set of pens on the north side. We finally reached St. Clair Public School. Bowes pulled the heavy Ford over sharp.

"Here?" Bowes snapped.

"Here," I replied.

I handed him a five and waved him to keep it. With a grunt, he passed back the receipt I requested yesterday.

"Thanks, dimple doll," he said just before he jumped out to open the back door for me.

I swung my legs over and out and puffed the air out of my lungs. I was on my own now. "Catch ya later."

Bowes motored off fast and made a sharp left turn at Runnymede Road despite the police car minding the call box. Too early to tick, or maybe a standing arrangement. St. Clair Public School was a small square with a brown brick dormer rested high above the front stairs. The wooden double doors bestowed the building with an institutional appearance rather than the neighbouring industrial. Windows pillared this formidable building all around except for the northern side. I speculated for a moment that the children needed clear views of the walled plants next door and the corrals beside and across the street, though I knew the glass was meant for letting in a little light. Through a gap in the schoolyard's fence, I skirted the edge of the pogey garden. In this diligently tended garden, 27 plots fit geometrically with tools, buckets and wheelbarrows lined up straight along the edges. As I passed, somebody familiar looking—I thought it was Mr. Dimitroff or maybe Mr. Copeland who lived on Britannia by Al's folks—looked up from his weeding, waved and shouted, "Hey, Red. Say hey to Al!" Just what a girl detective wanted to hear on her way to a stake out.

Invisibility was essential but next to impossible in a neighbourhood such as Al's.

NAKEV—AL'S VERSION

His ass hardly touched the bench. He bounced up, picked up a ball and drew a bead on the pins. He was a good bowler and the fluid delivery almost covered his reaching into the gutter and picking up a spring-loaded knife. The switchblade glinted in the brightness of the big fluorescent lights. Young Rep calmly got up from where he was sitting, casually picked up a bowling ball, walked up and dropped it on Nakev's foot. He then bent down and retrieved the dropped switchblade. Meanwhile, Navek was doing a dance on his good foot.

"Enough of this crap," said Cappie. "Siddown and sing for us."

"If I knew anything, I would have told ya already," said Nakev, who seemed to be recovering from the old bowling-ball-on-the-foot thing quite rapidly. Then I realized that the full force of the ball had been absorbed by the floor and only caught the edge of his foot.

"How often did Junior O see Kat?" I said, jumping right to what was supposedly the meat of the matter.

"They weren't dating," he said. "They met for coffee at the Double R in the afternoon, a couple of times a week. They barely spoke. He would give her an envelope before she left. Kat's a pretty good looking dish but she is real choosey. I took her out a couple of times when we were kids but since she matured I've asked her out many times. She wouldn't go for it. On those days when she met Junior O, I met her outside the restaurant and walked her back to the Mission. For this, Junior paid me a sawbuck a week."

"What was in the envelope?" I asked. It was a stupid question but, as this was a developing criminal matter, I couldn't make any assumptions.

"I never saw inside an envelope but when she dropped it once, I picked it up. Felt like maybe a wad of cash inside," he answered.

"Apart from his old man, where would he get a wad of cash he could turn over to Kat a couple of times a week?" I asked another obvious question

"Don't know," he shot back. His foot was obviously feeling better and he was getting annoyed with the questioning, "And I don't think his old man knows either."

"What was the money for?" I was running out of questions.

"I don't know. I asked Kat once and she told me to mind my own fucking business."

"She didn't use the 'F' word," I said, defending her without reason.

"I was there. You wasn't. Don't tell me what she did or did not say." He was close to losing his temper.

"You don't know where he got it. You don't know how much it was. You don't know what it was for. Hell, you don't even know for sure that it was cash," I said, to get him back on track.

"Don't complain about the answers when you're the one asking the stupid questions," he said, followed by a loud crack as the Young Rep slapped him hard across the face. His head recoiled and as it returned to its previous position, a trickle of blood ran from his nose. He dug around in his pockets, obviously trying to locate a handkerchief. Nobody offered him one. Finally, the pin boy gave him a paper napkin from the snack bar.

Cappie looked at the boy and politely said, "Get lost."

Being an intelligent kid, he did immediately.

I was surprised at this turn of events. Nakev being no real help was no surprise, but I had never seen any sign of unrest between members of the Maria Street Dark Boys' Association. The original group had all been Canadian-born progeny of Italian immigrants: handsome young men, with jet black wavy hair and flawless white skin. It was not possible or desirable to exclude anybody from the loosely organized group, which had no membership requirements and did not involve organized activities whatsoever. So, they added guys of different ethnic backgrounds: Polocks, Ukes, Czecks, Wasps, you name it. If you were male, kept your nose clean and lived on or near Maria Street, you had all the necessary qualifications for membership. The big thing was group support for members.

These boys knew their way around the Junction, particularly the western area, from the CPR station to the city limits, and the Brewers' In & Out store on the edge of York county at Jane Street, up and down from the south side of Annette Street to the city limits to the north, just beyond the stinking packing houses and the city garbage incinerator. I was surprised that no one knew anything about Junior O and the cash. I had no doubt that finding the amount and source of the money would lead to the motive for his murder and the murderer himself . . . or herself. One thing I was sure of was whatever it was, it was something far from honest. I wondered about Kat's involvement in something like that, and I could hear the words again: there were drifters and commuters, con men and crapshooters . . . .

MULLED IT OVER SOME–WILL'S VERSION

It was way past noon the next day when the door bell rang again. Past one and two o'clock as well.

"You're still not up?" asked Bobby, incredulous, not even trying to keep a straight face. I let him in anyway.

"Yeah well, I let a little old lady drink me under the table," I winced remembering Mrs. O's rather strong measures. "Forget it," I said, answering his puzzled frown.

"How was your ballet?" he asked as he gathered empty glasses and full ashtrays, automatically busing my living room. I had seen him do this so often I didn't even comment. He was a compulsively neat busy body. Bobby Busy Body. I ignored his query. Changed the subject.

"How was your show last night?" I asked. He ignored me right back. I watched him tidy up while I rolled us both a smoke. "Leave that," I handed him one and lit the other. "Let's walk down to Mars for a late breakfast," I pushed him gently, toward the door.

"Late lunch," he was smiling again.

We walked south to the deli. Winter was in the air with a vengeance. I felt under dressed in my tweed jacket, no overcoat, but Bobby was carrying his coat and seemed comfortable enough in his shirt sleeves. Bobby always struck me as feeling comfortable. I think he was the most comfortable man I ever met.

"Any word on that Junior thing?" he asked without looking at me. We settled ourselves in a too small booth at the back of Mars. I told him about Mrs. O's late night visit. He whistled through his clenched teeth—an absurdly musical whistle, of course.

"You believe her that she didn't send Roy your way?" I didn't answer right away. I figured I better decide what I believed first. I mulled it over some while we waited for my breakfast and Bobby's lunch.

"Not really sure," I admitted. "Wanna come visit Roy with me?" I began to butter an already pretty buttery piece of toast while watching Bobby's teeth show themselves in one of his patented hundred watt smiles.

"Could be interesting," he said.

KAT–AL'S VERSION

I went back to my room at the Y, changed into a good pair of gabardine slacks, a fresh shirt and a windbreaker. Even though it was quite early, I headed for the meeting with Kat. At Bloor and Dundas around 8 o'clock, I crossed to the southwest corner to stroll through the used car lot that was part of Puddicombe's Ford dealership. The staff had all gone for the day so I was able to stroll around without being annoyed by some dumb ass salesman. I did see a 1949 Meteor that I really liked but couldn't determine the price. While ostensibly looking at used cars, I studied the corners and the restaurant itself. I kept my eye on it all because, for reasons I could not explain, I felt uneasy.

About 15 minutes before our scheduled meeting, four young men that I could identify as fellow members of the Maria Street Mission's Softball Team got off a downtown bound streetcar and stood talking and laughing a little ways from the corner in front of former big league baseball player Goody Rosen's Dunsway Restaurant, which had opened recently. Goody established himself playing centre field for the Brooklyn Dodgers. It was quite an accomplishment as he was Canadian and Jewish, but what surprised me was the fact that not only did he bat left, he threw left. Throwing left-handed from the outfield was a handicap of sorts and for reasons I could never quite understand, lefties invariably put a curve on the ball when they threw it. It was a little difficult to throw accurately from centre field to home plate and cut down a base runner.

A few minutes after the boys arrived, Kat got off a Dundas streetcar and walked directly up to where they were standing. She spoke to them as if she was lecturing her Sunday school class. When she had finished, the group dispersed. Bonnie crossed the road to the corner dominated by the Canada Bread bakery, Lloyd stayed in front of the Dunsway, Dirtch crossed Dundas and Bloor and took up a position a little south of Fran's and Dimmie crossed to the corner closest to me. This was fortunate. Dimmie and I were close friends and were planning to drive to Florida in February with Pete and Cliff. I continued to meander around the used cars, but

88

stayed close to the corner, gradually making my way to the car closest to him.

"Don't turn around," I said, "I'm looking at the horrible green 1950 Mercury right behind you."

"It doesn't make any difference," he laughed. "I'm not going to beat you up, unless you get out of line with Kat."

"Why in the name of hell would I do that?" I asked, "And what do you mean by get out of line?"

"Well, she thinks since you're now a private detective, you're some kind of tough guy. When she told me, I almost bust a gut laughing. But I quickly realized she was serious and she figures if she can't tell you what you want to hear—which she can't—you'll be angry," he said without stopping to take a breath, "And she thinks that you and her are potentially a couple, if you know what I mean."

"I know what you mean," I groaned. "She sounds like she is really screwed up. Any idea why?"

"Nope," he said rather philosophically. "The Mission is having some financial trouble, but it always had financial trouble. How many times have we paid for our own softball hats and sweaters? Come to think of it, we've always paid for our hats and sweaters and none of us attend the church."

"Yeah," I mused intelligently. "Well, it's about time for me to check in. You hang out here, I'll go down the street, cross the road and come back on the other side. Has Dirtch got a knife with him? I haven't trusted him ever since he stuck Cappie in the washroom at the Double R."

"I don't know. I don't trust him either," he replied,

"I wouldn't have anything to do with him except he's a good outfielder and, as he says, he is now such a good Christian that he doesn't own a knife."

"Sure! Like I believe him," I said. "I'll talk to you later . . . do me a favour and make sure Kat gets home safely."

"Uh-huh," he said. Even though I could only see the back of his head, I knew he had a smirk on his face.

I walked west down Bloor to Indian Road, crossed the street and walked back up to the corner where Lloyd stood guard. I looked at him, smiled, nodded and he almost broke out laughing.

"How's Betty?" I asked.

"Fine," he said, "Planning the wedding is taking up a lot of her time and we are having trouble getting a suitable date at the church. I'll let you know when we do and you can keep the date open."

"Fine," I said, "Tell her I was asking after her."

"Yeah," he said.

It had become a custom for both bride and groom to round up as many single guys as they could to attend the wedding reception. The families at the wedding would have a preponderance of maturing single girl children. We were asked to show up, enjoy the free booze, have a good meal and enjoy an evening of dancing. As we grew into maturity, we found that we had to dance with more mothers every time somebody got hitched. The husbands just wanted to smoke, drink and talk about old times.

Crossing to the next corner, I got a smile out of the way Bonnie stood staring at the full moon so he didn't have to look me in the eye. He was embarrassed.

I waited for the traffic light to change with a small crowd of people and was able to mingle long enough for Dirtch to turn his back so I could sprint to the door and through it to the bright interior of Fran's. Kat was sitting about halfway down on the right with her back to the door. I slid into the seat opposite her and we both smiled. She was fashionably dressed in jeans and a blouse. Jeans were all the rage now. A pink sweater lay on the bench seat beside her. I was glad she wasn't wearing it as pink really gets to me.

A waitress came with menus, but neither of us needed one. Kat ordered a cherry coke. I ordered a grilled cheese sandwich, an order of french fries and a glass of milk.

"Look," I said, "Let's leave the personal stuff until Junior O's shooting is cleared up."

"You're sure he was shot to death?" she asked sweetly.

"A bullet hole in the gut is a pretty convincing piece of evidence," I said knowingly.

"Corinne the cosmetician who works for Lynette's Funeral Home says he was throttled," she informed me with an understandable hint of smugness.

"Did Corrie tell that to the coroner?" I asked.

"Tried but couldn't get anyone to listen," she said tilting her head down a little and looking up under her eyebrows at me, very seriously with her brown eyes.

"What was a cosmetician at Lynette's doing working on the body? Junior was Jewish, and their burial rites are different from mine."

"It's a family thing. It's what the family wants," she said knowingly. I let that sink in. "In any event," she continued, "She didn't actually see the body. The girl she works with did, and she told Corrie."

"Okay, okay. What was he paying you for and how much were you getting?" I asked in a rather demanding tone.

"He wasn't paying me and I don't know how much it was," she snapped.

At this point, the waitress put my sandwich and the fries on the table and took off toward the front counter to get my milk and Kat's coke mixture. Kat liberally salted my fries, picked one up and started to nibble.

"So how much was it, what was it for, and where was he getting it from?" I blurted, and not too professionally either.

Kat, now on her third chip, got very smug at this point and pointing her nose in the air said, "You're the private eye. I thought you knew all the answers!"

The waitress heard this as she put Kat's drink in front of her and stared at me with an air of incredulity as she put my milk down.

"Will that be all, sir?" she said with increased respect.

"Yes, that will be all," said Kat with that scratch-your-eyes-out tone that women seem to have that men don't. She then looked at me with a rather hard stare and said, "I've already told you I don't know how much it was. I don't know where he was getting it from, although I assumed it was coming from his father, and I don't know why . . . "she stumbled a little and looked at me helplessly.

"You'll feel better if you tell me about it," I lied.

"Alright," she said resolutely, "I received an envelope that I was quite sure contained money from Junior O twice a week. I delivered the envelopes unopened to the Reverend Jack. Ask him how much it was, what it was for, and why Junior was paying him if you wish, but leave me out of it. Please! Now if that is all, you can drive me home."

"I don't have a car," I admitted, rather embarrassed at this confession of penury, "But Dimmie will see you get home safely. I fixed it with him."

"No. Dimmie will not," She said frostily. "You are just as capable of taking a streetcar as he is and if you don't have enough for the fares, I'll lend you whatever you need to cover it."

Figuring I might catch Preacher Jack at the Mission and start getting a few answers, I dropped a tip on the table, paid the check and in the cool of the evening, with Kat hanging on my arm, boarded a Runnymede-bound Dundas streetcar. Kat had her cardigan on her shoulders, like a cape under her coat, and I immediately noticed that the pink went well with her brown eyes. She knew that, I was sure.

I felt a little down because I had accomplished nothing but I had moved along quite well. The Mission was short of cash which was nothing unusual. Kat had only been an unknowing conduit for, I assumed, money flowing from Junior O to Preacher Jack for reasons I was yet to determine and the biggest thing, Junior O had been murdered, yes, but not shot to death. He had been choked. No, not choked, throttled! Somebody did it with their bare hands. There was more emotion involved when a murder victim was throttled.

I walked Kat home from the end of the Dundas streetcar line, which left me a few houses down the street from where I would likely find Preacher Jack. I headed in that direction and as I did I could hear that damned tune: They wore fancy shirts and collars, but where they got their dollars . . . .

NO MOVEMENT AT NUMBER THIRTEEN—RED'S VERSION

Blakley Avenue was another road leading nowhere. Just above the pogey gardens, above the brush, Blakley's south end t-boned Henrietta. On my way through the brush, where the city put up the boards for the hockey rink and the pleasure rink, I saw a feral orange tabby in a frozen hunter's pose with her ears just above the tall grass. I hesitated. The cat caught the motion, slowly lowered to a four-legged squat and darkly watched as I walked on. Every living thing here is as tight as the skin on sausage.

Blakley's north end was a genuine dead end. Heavy dark boards were hammered together—a utilitarian but effective warning to automobile drivers of the steep ravine at the rail spur. The trains rode to the coal and paint plants and then back east to the yards west at Keele. A couple of dozen houses bravely occupied the southern half of Blakley against a herd of scrub, sumach and service berry. East of Blakley was the city's incinerator buildings with its attendant dump at the ravine's crevice. Rooting around in the crevice as a kid, Al found a hand grenade shell, which was later confiscated by his mother, unmoved as she was by his enthusiasm for discovery.

Some 20 years after the grenade find, I discovered the Winstanley's home at number 18 Blakley. 18 was one of those two-storey semi-detached working man's houses like the others in the neighbourhood. Al called William Winstanley and fixed it so I could sit on his porch or lean against its side, while I watched for the coming and goings of a certain boarder residing down a bit at number 13. After I reached 18's steps, I leaned on the railing post and looked past a young maple towards another working man's two-storey semi. Galvanized steel, seven-foot tall, separated the east side of the street's houses, backyards and sheds from the incinerator's edge. Symes' incinerator burned the city's trash, save for the tin, which was harvested after the war. Blackish smoke billowed mushroom-like from the two giant chimney stacks. Men still headed home from the plants either in groups or alone. When eyes were cast toward me, I waved and smiled, getting the odd nod in return before eyes were cast elsewhere.

Reading during a stakeout was forbidden, just like the sale of booze was forbidden in the Junction. You just had to know how and where to look. The fat squar-ish hardcover was set up between me and number 13 where my peripheral vision would catch the flutter of movement. Today's book was Invisible Scarlet O'Neil versus the King of the Slums. Either in a spirit of good will or as a playful taunt, Will bought me the Better Little Book that featured the first super heroine of the daily funnies, Invisible Scarlet O'Neil. Earlier this year, Will rooted around in Edward Warren's narrow Second Hand Books and Magazines Store and thumbed pages for hours with Edward's tacit consent. The store owner figured a passing customer was more likely to walk into a store with somebody already there. An added bonus for Edward, Will sprung for the odd book or magazine too. Will said Scarlet was just like me, except she was able to become invisible simply by pressing two fingertips on her left wrist. However, Will said even though her name is Scarlet, her hair was black. Maybe author Russell Stamm was a Vivien Leigh fan. In any event, I brought the book today because it fit in my purse and because, in a hopeless tone, Will asked on occasion if I have read it.

The stakeout was so long, I read the comic-like book three times. I liked the heroine Scarlet. Besides acting like a damsel in distress on occasion, she saved a municipal housing project by untangling a messy case—our female sleuth outsmarted the slum king, corrupt committee members and clueless architect. Between flipped pages, as Al advised, I knocked on the door of number 20 Blakley and requested a glass of water. An anxious middle-aged woman in a light flowered apron lightened considerably when I told her I was minding the Winstanley's house for a wire that might or might not be arriving today from England. Number 20 would be Mrs. Claire Dunn. Al said telephone party lines were hotter than telegram wires. When, and if, a neighbour made a telephone call to Mrs. Dunn about the young reader leaning on the porch, the word of my good deed would be repeated up and down Blakley, Henrietta and streets beyond.

Al had not told me why I was to follow this copper-haired headed man, just that I was to follow him. Not knowing why made it a bit harder as I did not know what I was to look for. I waited. Waited. Waited. Waited all day. In my notebook I wrote: 6:05 a.m.: Arrived at number 18 Blakley. No movement at Number 13. 7:00 a.m.: No movement at number 13. 8:00 a.m.: Spoke with Mrs. Dunn at number 20. 8:35 a.m.: Older woman wearing a dark green coat with dark skirt, approximately forty to fifty years of age, leaves Number 13 travelling south through the field beyond Henrietta. 8:45 a.m.: Four children run down the street, through the field to St. Clair Public School. 9:00 a.m.: No movement at Number 13. 9:45 a.m.: A young man, approximately 20 to 25 years of age, asks if he can help but leaves when I advise, "waiting on a wire". 10:00 a.m.: No movement at number 13. 11:00 a.m.: No movement at number 13. Noon: No movement at number 13. 12:30 p.m.: Mrs. Dunn brings a hot tea and egg sandwich. Kept conversation short and line of vision clear to Number 13. 1:00 p.m.: No movement at Number 13. 1:05 p.m.: Returned the cup and plate to Number 20. 2:00 p.m.: No movement at Number 13. 3:00 p.m.: No movement at Number 13. 3:15 p.m.: Suspect exits Number 13 by the back door. Mounts a red CCM bicycle.

I stuffed my notebook in my purse, pulled out a black tam, removed my brown scarf and replaced it with a navy one. Our suspect rode down the side walkway to Blakley and headed towards the field. I was panicked and afraid I would lose him, as I had not counted on the bicycle in this weather. But figured I would follow a little. He was as described: about 5'8", copper hair, round face, wire rimmed glasses, stocky build. He was wearing a dark pea jacket and grey pants, with a black mail bag slung over one shoulder. I thought that I must add this to my notes later: he was fast on a bicycle. I ran down Blakley to Henrietta, just in time to see him peel along the westerly foot path in the field towards Britannia Avenue. I broke into a trot, crossing Henrietta when I heard someone who eerily sounded like a British

Auntie Em calling "Dor-o-thy! Dor-o-thy!" Startled, I looked west. A short, slenderly hunched woman with warm brown hair was calling my name and waving. Al's mother was coming back from quilting at the Church of the Advent.

I looked back. My suspect was gone.

PREACHER JACK—AL'S VERSION

He occupied a small one-bedroom suite located behind the Mission building. It was furnished with odds and ends of used furniture. I wondered if Chaim the Junk Dealer provided most of it. A musty smell had settled in the suite, which was, no doubt, due to the fact that—like most men—he never thought to open a window to let the bad air out and the fresh air in. Of course, on Maria Street, one had to catch fresh air at precisely the right moment.

I told Preacher Jack that I had been talking with Kat and, rather than beat around the bush, asked him right out how much money was in the envelopes he got twice a week and why Junior O was paying him.

"I don't know how much was in the envelopes. I never opened one," he said, surprising me. "And, of course, I wasn't being paid for anything and to answer your next question, I don't know where Junior O was getting the money."

There was a long pause as I digested this information and before I could ask my next question, Jack volunteered, "Mind you, I will admit I received a modest delivery fee for passing the money along and I must say—from the thickness of the envelopes—I was quite sure it was a substantial amount."

"Delivered it to who?" was my next intelligent probe.

"I told you the other day when we spoke. Oh! Did I thank you for the lunch? It was really very nice of you, but I did tell you then that you should be talking to the neighbours up the street about this . . . did I not?" he lectured.

"Yes you did," I said, embarrassed by my own stupidity. If I had just listened more carefully to what he had said, I might have saved time and aggravation.

"Did you give the envelope to a specific person? Can you give me a name?" I pleaded.

"No. I simply dropped the envelopes in their office mail slot and went about my own business," he said.

After a long studied silence, he asked the next question, "Are you going to be seeing Kat socially?"

It was, after all, a logical question from someone who knew us and our individual status. If you can call living in a phone booth size room at the Y, eating irregularly and, except when visiting the folks for a few kind words and a home-cooked meal, grabbing greasy restaurant meals at irregular intervals, a status.

"No," I said, "We more or less agreed to let things sit until the murder of Junior O is resolved." On that note, I thanked him and, feeling claustrophobic, headed for the door.

I wanted to talk to Red about approaching the people at the Junction shul. When I got to Gilmour and Dundas, it struck me: none of us had spoken to Mr. O or Mrs. O. Although I had the brief encounter with Norbert O at the Vigor Oil office. Just something else I had better discuss with my partners. As I waited for the Red Rocket, I heard the damned song lyric—They wore fancy shirts and collars—and looked across the street at Mr. O's building. I wondered if I went in, would I find him wearing a fancy shirt and collar?

I heard a soft female voice speak my name, turned to see Kat standing next to the wall of Mr. O's building across the street and beckoning me over. I waited until the streetcar stopped in front of me and then sprinted around the rear of the car; I figured it would mislead some people into thinking that I had boarded. She didn't have a name, but she had learned that Junior O had been involved with one or more of the jockeys being suspended that summer for fixing races. This might open up a new avenue of investigation in the case. Having said what she had to say, she turned and disappeared around the corner.

I walked briskly to the Double R where I could use a payphone with some degree of privacy and called the Metropole. When the pump man who provided us with an answering service picked up the telephone, I almost screamed at him—I had waited for so long for someone to answer the phone. A few minutes later, Will came on the line and I made small talk until I was sure he wasn't slurring his words. I asked him if Red was also at the Met, but she'd just left—worked all day at her other job. I told him I had a new lead. He seemed more attentive now. I told him that one of the jockeys who had been ruled off for fixing races in the summer, and possibly others, had been involved with Junior O. I didn't tell him I was stretching things a bit or that I had picked this info up from Kat. He and Red didn't have a great deal of respect for Kat and had I mentioned her name, they may have written off the information.

Once again I crossed to the south side to board the Red Rocket and this time I did. Back to the Y. Tomorrow morning, we'll meet at the Metropole and talk things over with them so we could make some real progress. Time was flying, I thought. Then I thought of Eddie and his float equipped plane. That was one of the things we had to clear up.

MAN OF THE HOUR—WILL'S VERSION

Bobby and I strolled over to Spadina to look for the now erstwhile Roy Smith. Poking our heads into every poolroom and diner on the strip took an hour. There were a lot of them. We gave it up as a lost cause around 6 o'clock when B.B. reminded me that it was cocktail hour by his reckoning. For the man who mostly plied his trade in nightclubs, there were quite a few such hours. Bobby liked a drink or three, but was never the worse for it—especially not on the bandstand.

We sauntered over to his workplace at El Mocambo for the aforementioned cocktail. We had it, agreed that it was a fine cocktail, and had another. I'm certain that we would have eventually agreed that this new cocktail was also fine, except that the bartender called me to the telephone. It was Roy Smith, man of the hour.

"I heard you were looking for me," he sounded far away and muffled.

"I am looking for you. Why'nt you come here for a chat?" The bartender, Jimmie Tap, was pretending to polish a beer schooner—staying close and listening.

"You got any news on that item we were talking?" he sounded even more faint now. I was about to answer when he let out a sort of gasp and the line went dead.

Funny thing, his sort of a gasp wasn't faint at all.

NOVEMBER 16, 1951

METROPOLE SUMMIT NUMBER THREE—AL'S VERSION

Great pub fare for breakfast this morning. Red was not happy that I took her off the Blakley assignment, nor with my suggestion that she interrupted as rousting the people at the Junction shul. It took me quite a long while to explain that we were not going to roust anyone. We knew a least one person was receiving a fat envelope of money and had a few simple questions. How much was it? What was it for? She seemed unconvinced; I didn't pursue it. I knew eventually we would have to ask someone, but decided to let her think about it. Will still liked Edwin Boyd, or one of Boyd's associates, for the murder but wasn't making much progress in that regard, and in fact felt that we couldn't pin Junior O on them. I felt odd about the Mrs. O visit. Red and Will seemed distracted this morning, but we headed out for sleuthing anyway.

BEFORE AND AFTER SUMMIT NUMBER THREE—RED'S VERSION

More embarrassed than offended that Al took me off the Blakley cooper-headed man stake out, yet relieved he did before Will arrived, I considered my options. My other job was a telephone operator at Maxwell's Oracles at the Temple-Pattison Building around the corner on College Street. It was as slow as a clock's little hand, but one takes what one can get. A shift or two a week helped pay the rent on my current abode. I thought I was finished with working two jobs when I landed at Al and Associates, but that was not to be. At Lloyd George Apartments, except for the odd clandestine visit by Morrie the superintendent, no one rummages through my place. The landlords of my Humberside flat occasionally exposed their visits by moving items—a bottle of beer for example—out of a cupboard and placing it in plain view on my tiny kitchen table. These days, the odd beer in my apartment is secure but the price for a securely closeted bottle was higher rent. One may buy privacy, but privacy meant holding two jobs. Besides, I squirrelled away twenty dollars a month for my future ladies' beer parlour, The Corner Pocket. Answering phones and delivering messages a couple shifts a week at Maxwell's Oracles was a smart choice for a single girl. Working with Al Green and Associates was the odd one. My detective cases felt like the breezes in Tweed.

After this morning's summit, I called Detective Old and left a message with an unenthusiastic officer that I would drop by soon. Next, I called the International Ladies and Garment Workers' Union, more specifically one of their organizers, Sarah Pope. I worked with Sarah on Temple's campaign in 1948. Raised on Maria Street, her connections bolstered that CCF campaign bringing women and young people with her as well. Back in 1948, many women new to political campaigning gravitated towards her, including me. Sarah taught organizational skills with a combination of chutzpah and grace. Sarah was a young woman who could hold her own in the predominately boy's game of politics. Celebrated for her local popularity and organizational skills and noticed by the CCF brass, she stayed true to her roots. In the end, though Sarah was courted, she stuck with her union. Families were migrating to Toronto's north end, but Sarah stayed on Maria.

Back in 1948, one lesson Sarah taught was never duck the hard stuff. Deal with the problem. The longer you ignore a cut, the messier the infection. Deal with the hard task and move onto an enjoyable one. My calls from the Metropole house telephone this morning were to Old and Sarah. Though I didn't tell her over the phone that we had a question or two about the shul. Al needed to know why the money was being ferried to the Junction shul by Preacher Jack, or by Kat, or by Junior O. Who was the recipient? The money holds the key to Junior's murder, he argued, money's a motivator. I wondered about Al's rationale. If we relied on his questionable sources, we might offend members of the shul. Still, I knew enough to know if two sources said the same thing in a murder case, you best investigate. Sarah may know or may not know about the drops but, if it's happening at all, she would know who would know.

Al mistook my reluctance as squeamishness. Whispers of a connection between illegal bookmaking and the Junction shul were only for Maria Street. A loud mouthed question regarding any kind of financial transaction between the preacher and the Junction shul, or the son of Mr. O and the Junction shul, would be denied. However, the oddity of the Mission's preacher strolling easterly along that long curving street and slipping a big brown envelope of cash in the shul's mail slot once a week must be the talk of Sarah's block. Furthermore, a tension existed between the Maria Street Mission and the shul. The shul came first at the turn of the century; the Mission was built next. Many a storyteller recalls outdoor Sunday choir hymns on Maria Street or of needed food and work surreptitiously linked to mission service attendance. But why was the preacher ferrying drops of cash?

Fortunate for me, Sarah was direct in conversation. Sarah was in late this morning, she would meet me at the Lyceum. Fortunate for me, Sarah was direction in conversation. Neither of us ducks the tough stuff.

"SQUIRE . . ." HE SAID PLEASANTLY – WILL'S VERSION

Bobby and I had no luck with our queries into the whereabouts of Green and Associates' temporary employer, Roy Smith. I was worried, especially after our telephone conversation had been so abruptly terminated. No one would admit to having seen him, going on two days now. I was beginning to think that Smith wasn't even a Jewish name.

Seriously though, what, or more problematically, who was responsible for cutting us off?

Bobby was waiting for me at our rendezvous, Mars Deli, again. We'd poked around on our own the day before, covering twice as much ground by splitting up, or so we had thought. One look at each other was all it took to instantly know we'd had no better luck alone.

"Squire . . ." he said pleasantly tucking into a huge plate of griddle cakes. Bobby's appetite was like every other facet of his makeup: superior and rarefied.

We sat across from each other. Defeated.

TEMPEST IN A TEAPOT—AL'S VERSION

John the waiter said there was a phone message. I borrowed the bar phone and picked up the handset. Cappie had called to tell me that things were getting nasty. Last night, Young Rep got beat up and Cappie himself took a few blows. We agreed to meet at the Double R in an hour's time. No time to fill in my partners, I left first for the Sterling Tower and retrieved the office gun, only to realize we didn't have any ammunition to load it. I took it with me anyway.

I caught a Long Branch bound Queen streetcar over near Shea's Hippodrome and got off at Manning. I was a few steps away from Claremont Confectionery, Smoke and Gifts (with a Complete line of Guns and Fishing Tackle) at 720 Queen Street West. I legged it back along Queen to Bathurst Avenue, used the transfer I got going east to get me on the Bathurst car and later, the Dundas car headed west. Like a kid with a new toy, I couldn't wait. Seated more or less on my own, I broke the seal on the box of .32 pistol ammunition and loaded the Ivor Johnson.

I arrived at the Double R earlier than expected. My rushed arrival impressed the Maria Street Dark Boys Association members. They were even more impressed when they noticed the Ivor Johnson .32 which I had in a shoulder holster under my windbreaker. Word would spread quickly; Al Green was packing. The shoulder holster was very uncomfortable and the weight of the cartridges foolishly loaded into the chambers made the whole thing twice as heavy. I knew I would have a sweat rash in my left armpit area when I got home and I hoped I had some talcum powder in my room at the Y. I would not ask one of my effeminate neighbours if I could borrow some talcum powder, and the athletic straights on the floor would say that real men don't use talcum powder.

One glance revealed the Boys were raging mad and one eavesdrop revealed they blamed Mr. O for the violence visited upon their member, Young Rep. They had been looking for Nakev, as the action seemed to be retribution for the deviated septum Nakev blamed on Young Rep. I borrowed George's telephone book and checked the white pages to see if the Nakev family was listed. They were. I made a note of the number, handed the book back to George and asked if I could use his phone. Normally he'd tell me to use the pay phone but he was anxious to get the Boys calmed down and—if they were not going to buy anything —wanted them out of his restaurant.

I dialed the Nakev family number and asked for him. His mother told me he wasn't home. When I told her I was a friend, she confided to me that he was visiting a lady friend for a few hours. After thanking her, I dialed Kat's number. I told Kat that having another guy hang around her place was not doing a hell of a lot for our romance.

She snickered and said, "Say it with flowers!"

Before I could say anything more, Kat said Nakev looked like a raccoon with his two black eyes and swollen nose stuffed with surgical cotton.

"He's just waiting until the mob cools off and goes home," she said, and added with another chuckle: "You can come over and act as second chaperone if you wish."

"If I come over, he gets out," I said in my most brisk manner and then, as an afterthought, I asked, "What do you mean a second chaperone?"

"The reverend was kind enough to visit earlier," she said.

She was chuckling again as I was swearing mildly. I almost hung up when a thought came to me.
"Sneak a peek at the good reverend's hands and tell me if he has split or skinned his knuckles."

She wasn't chuckling anymore. She refused to do it but then, reluctantly after a pause, uttered, "No! They're fine, you animal." And Kat hung up.

I looked at Cappie accusingly. He was present when the violence erupted and in fact had a part in it. He was generally a jovial sort, but when aggravated he could hold his own with the best of them. The majority of them had heeded George's words and were now comfortable in booths, sipping or munching something. I used my head as a signalling device to tell Cappie to step outside. I slipped out and only waited a couple of minutes before he stepped out; we stood quietly looking at each other.

Finally, I broke the silence. "What happened?"

He changed feet a couple of times and spilled, "Young Rep wanted another go at Nakev and I told him to cool it. Nakev had more than enough. Young Rep wouldn't listen. Said something about being embarrassed in front of you by not laying him out. I told him it didn't matter, but Rep been into his old man's whisky. I had to get a little physical."

"I'm sorry, Cappie. There's no need for him to be embarrassed, but when he gets it in his head, well, you can't change it," I said. "Where is he now?"

"St. Joseph's emerg," Cappie said. He referred to the only hospital convenient to the Junction.

"Can you cool his boys off?" I asked hopefully.

"Yeah," he said. "Sorry to get you involved in this."

"Makes me feel wanted," I said. We shook hands, which is what we jocks are supposed to do.

Cappie was on his way back inside and I was walking away when George stuck his head out the door to tell me I was wanted on the telephone.

"I tell ya, it is hell to be popular," I muttered as I stepped in behind Cappie.

Kat was calling on the house phone. When she spoke, she sounded like she had been crying so I was wary. Women often do this as a ploy to get their own way about whatever they want their own way about.

"I'm sorry," she said sounding sincere. "I wasn't very nice to you on the telephone earlier, and I had no reason to be that way. Are we still more than just friends?"

I hesitated. This is the point where most guys put their foot in it and I was one of the guys.

After some thought on my part she said, "Al? Are you still there?"

Having thought it through, I decided I was, in fact, still there. "Yeah! Don't worry about it. Everything will work out okay. Unfortunately, the florist is closed or I'd send you some red roses to cheer you up," I finished.

"They'll be open tomorrow," she said.

I'd put my foot in it in a way, regardless of all the thought. Guys just can't win at this game. "You can send Nakev home. The danger, if there really ever was any danger, has passed. I'll call you," I said and hung up.

I crossed the road and went into the Runnymede Pharmacy on the northeast corner. Schreiber was the only pharmacist on duty. "Do you do urinalysis?" I asked with a straight face.

"Certainly," he replied. "This is a full service pharmacy."

"Well, wash your hands, I want an ice cream cone." I laughed. He didn't.

The only thing they had was the popular mello-roll type. A roll—equal to a scoop and a half of ice cream—was individually wrapped, and carefully unwrapped, by a certified pharmacist, and slipped into a common wafer cone. They only came in three flavours: vanilla, strawberry and chocolate. I swear that if you were blindfolded you couldn't differentiate the taste of one for one of the others.

"How is your case going?" Schreiber asked. "First aid supply sales have gone up sharply quite recently. Gauze rolls for nosebleeds, tincture of iodine, Mercurochrome, adhesive tape and much more!"

"Do I qualify for a kickback?" I asked.

"You've already got a free ice cream cone and I tolerated your stupid joke. I think we're even," he smiled.

"Hardly quid pro quo," I observed.

"Yeah," he said. On that note, I left.

Using the same transfer I had picked up when I

had left the office, I boarded the bus heading north on Runnymede. The driver looked at the transfer and the time issued. He then looked at me with a stern look that people who have adopted a sense of authority and was about to say something when I started a detailed description of the various delays, missed connections and short-term cars. Before I finished, he closed the doors and went on our way.

I smiled inwardly and hummed the line Con men and crapshooters! There's a little bit of larceny in us all.

TALKING WITH SARAH— RED'S VERSION

This morning, the hot water actually filled the claw foot tub. I soaked for a while. The heat soothed my sore back from the stake out. Once soaked, bathed, shampooed and dressed, I opened the frosted foot square window between the bathroom and the kitchen, and left the bathroom door open to let the steam add moisture in the arid apartment. Breakfast in the galley kitchen consisted of tea, a piece of fried bacon and a single egg complemented by a slice of bread fried in the remains of the bacon fat. I would ask Morrie to unclog the back burner jet; the jet snubbed the match again. Tomorrow, I vowed, I would defrost the freezer, preventing ice crystals from sealing tight the aluminium freezer. Despite the white and green quilt straightened on my bed, and because the curtains were pulled across the front bay window, Toronto's soberness controlled the room. A dust of snow covered the front yards across Huron, but merely wet the sidewalk and street. More snow fell. Trees with missing leaves endured the moist, windy cold day. I grabbed my winter garb and stuffed a notepad in my purse. I ventured out after a rattle of the doorknob. I overheard the twins living across the hall bickering again about who's wearing whose dress. As if there was a difference. Further down the hall, I paused at Pam Esson's door but, hearing nothing, I passed. She was probably working anyway. We would talk another day. I trotted down the arthritic switchback stairs.

I rushed along Huron, turned at Cecil past the Ostrovtkzer shul and left on Spadina. A block or two down, I crossed and climbed the steps to the Labor Lyceum. Inside, the International Ladies and Garment Workers' Union office door was open. Sarah was talking on the telephone, but gestured as I walked in and held an index finger up signalling me to wait a minute. We both smiled as she finished the call.

"Well, if it isn't big Dottsy Brophy . . . how you been?" Sarah jumped out of her chair and reached up for a hug. "Don't say anything. Let's get out of here, I'm dying for a sweet. Sadie, I'm out for half an hour," Sarah shouted behind her to Sadie, who was form-filling at her desk.

Throwing a coat and scarf on, she linked her arm through mine. She stopped, cocked her head and rumpled my hair, "You don't change do ya? Ladovsky's okay for you? Close by. Coffee's good. Oops, you drink tea, don't cha?" She did not need an answer. We passed a few stores and walked in United Bakery's front door. Hellos and whistles from customers and staff rose as she was noticed in the door. Sarah laughed and waved back to the small room.

"Hey, Rosie," Sarah said. "How about a place at the end of the table? I need to talk to my girlfriend."

Rosie nodded, walked down and set two places by

the oven. Five minutes passed as Sarah chatted and joked with people, mostly in Yiddish, along the way to the table's end. She introduced me as her "CCF friend" to J.B. Salsberg, labour-progressive provincial member of parliament for St. Andrews, who in turn inquired after Bill Temple's campaign. I confessed I was not involved and Salsberg invited me to join his then. Once at our seats, Sarah ordered two coffees—hers was black—and cakes. I can drink coffee, but only unenthusiastically. She took out a pack of Lucky Strikes, lit one and tossed the match in the ashtray.

"Why are you mixed up with that dreck, Dorothy? Steve says you and some thin guy were handing out hand rolled cigs and asked the packing boys 'bout Junior O. Heard you met with the cops too. Word is Big Daddy, or Old Man or whatever his name is, is raising eyebrows all the way from Keele to Runnymede on both sides of the tracks with his bully boy tactics and friends. Why you working with these rinky-dink Pinkertons?" Sarah leaned back and took a long drag off her Lucky. Small talk was for mice. The coffee arrived.

"We're not Pinkertons, for Christ's sake." One day, I should stop prickling when provoked.

"Take your word on the first part. And the last part too," she said as she took another drag followed by a sip of coffee.

"Sarah, stop. Hear me out. Junior O is on our scope, but no one else's, and someone killed Junior. He may not have been a Massey or worker, but he doesn't deserve his murder unsolved. Suspects abound, but we need to narrow in on why someone actually pulled the trigger. We figure this out through talking to people on loading docks or coffee shops. Can I talk to you?"

"Ain't that what you're doing?"

"Yeah. Guess it is. Can I run a wild one by you?" I steadied myself.

"Sure. I wanna find out what's wild in Dot Brophy's eyes," she rubbed her cheek on her shoulder.

"You taught me never to duck the hard stuff. This is hard for me, but I'll say it anyway. We heard Junior O drops a whack of cash at the shul once a week. Also, heard Preacher Jack drops it over for him. That's wild," I sit back.

"Dot, you amaze me. Junior's piddly money is wild? How about the profit a garment factory makes off its workers? I call that wild."

"Sarah, I get it. You win. The good fight . . . I support it. You know it. But there's a local killer out and about. Anything you know about the shul drop offs would help." I stepped back from begging. Fortune intervened again.

"Yeah, I heard about it. My mother watches out the front window for the preacher passing by on Tuesdays and Thursday afternoons. Never misses. He's a bit puffy about it all. Like he's marching on to something. But it happens. Gives my mother something to talk about." More smoke, more coffee.

"Know who gets the money and what for?"

"Nope. Not really. Heard the gossip though. The envelope lands there and quickly leaves there. Rumour is half goes to support Junior's illegitimate daughter, a Corktown girl in the family he got way last year. The other half straight into a Dundas Scotiabank account. Rumour is a thousand a month. But you know, you're not asking the real question."

"I'll bite. What's the real question?"

"Where's Junior getting the cash?"

"Where was Junior getting the cash, you mean?"

"Now you win on tense. You're good with English, Miss Dorothy. But there's definitely a bigger question. Listen. Junior was careful not to be seen depositing either on Dundas or in Corktown. Using the preacher was a clever touch, except for the gossip it spawned. Never underestimate the legs on a bloated story. Hey, Junior was never the sharpest tool in the box. Maybe Junior got tired of being Sugar Ray Robinson. Wanted to get it on his own. Wanted to get out of the Junction. Everybody else seems to be fleeing the place. But he was saving because he was making. He made money somehow—stealing, extorting, betting—something fine, I'm sure."

At the words 'I'm sure,' Sadie flew in, controlled panic personified. Sarah stood and Sadie raced over, whispered in Sarah's ear and, with one motion, Sarah grabbed her coat and scarf. "You're buying eh, Dots? Trouble at one of the plants, I gotta run."

"Sure, thanks Sarah, anything else?" I turned on my chair and watched her go.

She stopped, "Oh, I don't know. The O boys scrapping pretty hard recently. Not hard enough to bring in the cops, but close to it."

"Thanks, will I see you on the 22nd?"

"Nah. Working for J.B. this time. Doesn't seem the same anymore with the old gang. Bye, Dotty. Don't be a stranger!"

Sarah was gone.

I sauntered up to the cash register and recited our order. It was on the house.

MESSAGE FOR MR. O – AL'S VERSION

I got off the bus at Cobalt Avenue and walked back to the Vigor Oil station. My old buddy, Bobby Walker, was working the pumps, though now he was pouring motor oil into a 1950 streamlined sky blue Studebaker. I recognized it as being the one owned by storekeeper Jimmy Evan, although it was his son Alex who was driving it now, obviously on his way to some kind of band job. Evan had his bull fiddle wedged into the car at an odd angle.

Evan ignored me as I passed, but Bobby smiled and said, "Yeah, the boss is in and the Brothers Assholeminov are up there with him."

"This should be fun," I replied.

"If you need any help with those two, just yell and I'll be there quick. They seem to have been born with some magic talent for getting under your skin," he said.

"If you are a frequent bettor, they will be really nice to you," I said, waxing philosophical.

"Don't use your heater around this place. The fumes here will ignite quickly with the hot gas from so much as one discharged cartridge," Bobby was giving me the benefit of his expertise.

"You speaking from experience?" I smiled.

"Seen it. Never did it," he smiled back.

I went up the stairs one at a time, and even though I had been forewarned, I made sure the Iver Johnson was loose in the holster.

At the top of the stairs, the door to the office was

open about a couple of inches, but it was enough for me to see Norbert O standing next to a seated Eddie. Eddie was bent over the papers on his desk, or just keeping his head down in anticipation of the coming festivities. Knowing that the other brother was in the office, it didn't take a genius to figure he was concealed behind the door. I did the logical thing, instead of shoving the door open, I pulled the door shut. Surprised, Izzy O took hold of the inner doorknob and started to gently open the door. His weight was now forward on his feet rather than balanced, so when I rammed the door with my shoulder, Izzy got a face full of plank. Stunned, he backed into the wall behind him with considerable force, then took an involuntary step forward and then, with the wall for support, slid down to a stunned sitting position.

Norbert O watched his brother with considerable disbelief. He should have been concentrating on me, but he hadn't expected Izzy to lose the first round. I took advantage of the distraction, stepped forward and launched a right hand shot into his face, catching him square on the bugle. It was taps for Norbert O, which was a good thing. Unlike Junior, they were big boys, carrying a lot of extra weight. I dragged one, and then the other to the top of the stairs and then just half-pushed, half-threw them down the stairs. Bobby Walker heard the racket and had come to make sure things were even. Obligingly, he dragged them one at a time outside so they were as close to their big, black Buick as they could be. Walker and Eddie grinned ear-to-ear, but being a professional person, I maintained my composure. Well, I guess I did allow myself a brief grin, realizing the word would get out that the private eye Al Green had taken on the two O bothers at the same time and kicked their asses. From now on, people would not try to get tough with me or any one of my partners.

I turned my attention to Eddie, who was still smiling at the spectacle of the O boys getting their lumps. I noticed a straight razor on the floor, and as I stooped to pick it up, I saw that I had a horizontal cut in my left trouser leg, halfway between the hip and the knee. The blade had nicked me and blood trickled down my leg. Eddie quickly got an adhesive bandage out of his first aid kit and taped a piece of gauze over the cut.

"You'll need a stitch or two," he said seriously.

"Got a needle and thread handy?" I joked.

"Go down to the emergency room at St. Joe's and they'll fix you up. Otherwise, you'll be dribbling blood all over everything for a long time. That cut is in a spot that stretches or contracts every time you move your leg. Get it closed properly, then you can buy a new suit and send Mr. O the bill. He will not be happy with his boys as it is. Having to outfit the guy that knocked them around in a new set of threads will really get up his nose." At this point he stopped to take a breath and I jumped in.

"You own an aeroplane. On floats yet. Can I see the log books?" I spoke plainly.

"Sure," he said, "But they're with the plane presently parked at the island airport. It's on floats. I keep it there from time to time. It's in Orillia the rest of the time. When Highway 400 is finished and opened up officially, I'll probably keep the kite in Orillia all the time. I'll phone the island and tell them you're coming. Park your car behind Maple Leaf Stadium in Little Norway and take the ferry across the western gap."

Little Norway was a reference to the World War Two barracks that had been used by Norwegian and other pilots in training who were learning how to fly. Or not fly. The picturesque airport was officially an Initial Training School. I was a baseball nut and frequently watched the baseball Leafs. Sitting in the stands, it was impossible not to notice the peculiar structures behind the right field fence and billboards which constituted the Little Norway barracks.

I decided the prudent thing was to see to the cut. I took the streetcar down Roncesvalles Avenue and got off when we reached Queen Street. I was going to nip into the Edgewater Hotel's pump room for a couple of quick draughts but thought better of it. I did one smart thing. I stepped into a phone booth and called my bookie, Bert D, to ask him if he could come down to St. Joe's and hold my hand while I awaited the skills of the seamstress. I didn't bet very often, but when I got a tip on a horse it was at a time when getting to the track was virtually impossible. Someday the provincial government would wake up to the fact that if they legalized off-track betting, they would reap a harvest of tax that presently was going into the bookies' pockets.

"I'm at St. Joe's emergency. I need some information," I explained to Bert D.

"Of course you do," he said with a hint of sarcasm. "I always go to one emergency or another to get information from my bookmaker. I'll be there shortly."

I walked west down Queen Street passing the gaping entry to the streetcar barns and another block got me to the hospital entrance. The nurse behind the front desk took my information and told me to have a seat. I didn't have any choice. Bert D came through the door. I was amazed how quickly he made the trip, but he was quick to explain that he had bought himself a 1949 Pontiac Stratochief. This was the car that confused American mechanics when you stopped to get the oil checked on a trip into the States. It was a Canadian version of a Pontiac but it had a Chevy straight six engine. They didn't sell them in the States, but they were very popular at home because that engine seldom needed repair work.

I quickly gave him a rundown of my recent dust-up with the O brothers and he chuckled appreciatively. Then he asked the direct question, "What do you want from me?"

"Well, there was a problem with a jockey not so long ago, and I don't remember the details," I said as nicely as I could.

"Ha!" he roared drawing a rather black look from the nurse behind the reception counter. "The Ontario Racing Commission suspended so many boys, the owners and trainers had to scratch nags because they didn't have riders."

"When was that?" I asked, interested to say the least.

"I don't know how long they had been working on it, but it was in August when they started to clean house. Some boys got thrown in the can, some got suspended for life. 10 or 12 were involved. It was in the papers. Don't you read?" he laughed.

"I remember something about it, but it didn't get the continuing coverage you'd expect it to attract. A lot of jockeys bit the dust, so to speak. I think the Racing

Commission sat on it as much as they could," I tried to recall details.

"Right. As soon as they suspected something was wrong, they went to work but there wasn't a peep in the papers until they started throwing kids in the can," Bert said.

"How did they catch on to the fact that something was wrong? I mean it's hard to spot, isn't it?" I asked, wanting something I could work with.

"The word is, and it was mentioned in the newspapers, a lady in black made a huge across-the-board bet on a horse in one of the races at Fort Erie. Like one or two grand, win, place, and show, and that is like taking out an ad in the Saturday Evening Post! They started investigating. They never did find out who she was, but they sure put the arm on a lot of the riders."

"Maybe it was Eddie Taylor in drag," I suggested and Bert howled.

A nurse called my name. I thanked Bert, got up and headed towards the examination room. Before I went, I knew I would not get a local anaesthetic but, with my trousers down below my knees, I was painfully surprised when the nurse disinfected the area with iodine before proceeding. She placed a surgical tray beside the stretcher-like table on which I was lying at such an angle that I couldn't see what was in it. A young intern walked quickly into the room, inspected the cut and then produced a piece of purple dyed catgut about a yard-and-a-half long with a built-in needle which was shoved painfully through the flesh of my leg from a half inch below the cut to about the same distance above it. Almost the entire length of the catgut was pulled through

122

my leg and tightened so as to pull the edges of the cut together. The half inch that was not pulled through my, leg was then used with the remaining yard-and-a-half to tie a complicated surgical knot. The significance of the knot escaped me. With the catgut pulled and tied, a set of surgical scissors were used to cut off the excess catgut.

Now I realized that everything used in tying the first stitch had been discarded and new catgut was produced from a cellophane package, a second stitch was made, a "surgical knot" tied, and another set of surgical scissors produced to cut off the excess cat gut. I couldn't believe the waste. It was compounded when a third stitch was deemed necessary and new supplies produced to finish the job.

I looked at the young intern, thanked her and said, "Now I can put my trousers on and go home?" This is an old joke.

She wasn't to be outdone. She smirked, "A couple of inches higher, a little to your right and you would have been circumcised."

"It would have been a miracle," I smiled. "Seeing as how my optimistic parents had that done before they knew how long it was going to be."

The smirk was gone. She turned and walked out, leaving me thinking how the tailored look of the all-white uniform made her and the nurse look more attractive than they really were. The white got me thinking of the lady dressed in black and not liking the thought of who she might be.

Bert was waiting for me; he said I owed him six bucks as he had paid for my stitches. Knowing I would be hungry, he handed me a hot dog liberally coated with mustard and loaded with onions. I was starving and with my mouth full of my first bite, I thanked him. "Come on, let's go. I'll drive you to wherever you're heading," he said. He didn't realize it but in an innocuous way, he was convincing me that I should buy a car. It would save a lot of time studying case notes on the streetcar.

"Where to?" he asked.

"West Toronto Junction," I said and climbed in.

WE WATCHED HIM GO—WILL'S VERSION

"I've got him spotted!" Bobby's voice was mellifluous and calm on the telephone. I was in what was beginning to seem like an annex to my apartment. Back to Mars.

"Crest Grill," he continued. "I'll try and hold him, but you should hurry."

I trotted down the couple of blocks from Bathurst to College. Roy was there, all angry. He was in the midst of writing what turned out to a cheque made to Green and Associates for our services. Services, which apparently, Roy had no further use for.

"I'm square with you guys, so lay off. Tell your boss Green especially!" Roy sputtered. "I hired you to look into things. Discreetly. And not talk to Mrs. O. What part of that did you stick to?!"

He was getting pretty loud. Barney, the grill man, was looking over. I interrupted his rant.

"Hell, we got your mystery all solved," I began.

"Don't tell me! We're square and now it's nothing to do with me," he looked around the diner a little frantically. I noticed how he had tissue paper stuffed up each nostril. Must have had a nose bleed. Must have needed B.B.'s persuading before he'd waited for me, I guess.

"I don't wanna know. You don't work the case for me. Can't you see that Al's breaking up the O's office on my dime, means I broke it up? I hadda leave town. I see now I came back too early," he slid his chair back, got up and left.

B.B. and I let him go. We watched him go.

AN EVENING WELL SPENT—AL'S VERSION

While I had been getting stitched-up Bert was busy. He filled me in as he drove. Young Rep had been treated and released. He wasn't as badly hurt as appeared when he was admitted. Izzy and Norbert O were being held for observation in the downtown Mount Sinai hospital on Yorkville Avenue. While Izzy had a broken collarbone from either his encounter with the plank or the flight of stairs, Nobby had a concussion. At the very least, the O brothers were slowed for the week ahead. As we rode in Bert's car, he ran down his remembrances of the summer horse racing scandal. A number of jockeys had conspired to fix the results of a number of races. At least two jockeys had been arrested and faced criminal charges while seven or eight others had been suspended indefinitely. After he rattled off the names of the accused, I felt badly as three of the boys I knew personally. I wondered if they had actually been a part of a conspiracy or if they had been coerced, one way or the other.

Bert drove north on Parkside Drive and Keele Street, turned west on Dundas Street and turned south at Pacific Avenue. This was the end of Bert's free taxi and news service. I told him that I appreciated his help and that I owed him, and he replied, "Yeah, hope I never have to collect." He then took off.

The lights were still on in Lewis Menswear Store which didn't surprise me as I had called Mrs. Lewis earlier telling her of my desperate need for a pair to match my suit jacket, plus a new suit. I never owned two suits in my life before and I was particularly happy knowing I was going to stick Mr. O with the bill.

Solly Lewis and I had been in the same Western Tech class and his older brother Bill was a couple of years ahead of us. Bill was annoyed when I purchased my first pair of tailor-made drapes from Mr. Huggins on Runnymede Road. Afterwards, I went to his family's outlet in the Junction. I was well looked after. Mrs. Lewis met me at the door and handed me a new pair of slacks identical in colour to the ones I was wearing, although a little larger in the waist and longer in the legs. A set of index cards were kept after you made your first purchase, a card bearing your name and address added to their index with measurements recorded and updated at the time of your next purchase.

I was in and out of the change room in no time at all and then she looked at the slit in the left leg of the ones I was wearing, discreetly ignoring the blood. Mrs. Lewis said their tailor would look at the slit, see if it could be invisibly mended and, if so, she'd have it cleaned and mended. She then handed me a bill for the new slacks and the suit which I would be able to pick up in about a week's time.

"Pay what you can, when you can," she said with her Jewish accent.

"Thank you," I said. "Tell Saul I was in and asking for him. I assume he is doing well?"

"He could work harder," she said, "But he will be pleased learning you are doing well. He was saying the other day that it is only time before you put the big bookmaker out of business."

"I doubt that'll happen," I responded as I moved toward the door. "I just want to catch Junior's murderer so his mother will have the satisfaction of knowing it's been done."

I knew she was right behind me and, having opened the door to leave, I turned and gave her a hug. She expected but appreciated the hug nonetheless.

"Shalom," I said softly, which got me a soft pat on my cheek, a warm smile and a soft "Shalom" in response.

As I walked away, the lights in the store switched off, confirming the kind lady had been waiting for me to arrive before retiring for the day.

I started back along Dundas Street but crossed the road to Dalton's Fur Store when I saw Jeanne and her daughter Sue standing outside, obviously waiting. Waiting for someone named either Ernie or Jack Dalton who, by the way, were both world-class fencers. Ernie had represented Canada as a member of the fencing team at the 1932 Summer Olympics in Los Angeles and the 1936 Summer Olympics in Berlin. In addition, Ernie was a landscape artist who spent his early years with the Group of Seven. He was also a pistol marksman of some repute. Jack was a fencing champion too. He held the Canadian Sabre Championship and became the Canadian Fencing Champion by defeating his father.

Back to Dalton Furs. When the family sedan pulled up

in front of the store, Jack got out of the passenger seat to open the rear door for his wife and daughter. Ernie, the father, was driving and I slipped around to the driver's side where he had obligingly rolled the window down. He immediately recognized the bulge on my left side where the .32 was holstered.

I quickly asked, "I need someone to teach me how to use this Iver Johnson. Can you help me?"

He immediately responded, "You need a license to carry. Get it from the police. But first of all, get rid of that antique. Check the yellow pages and pick out a conveniently located gun club. They'll give good advice on the license and, once you've got it, they'll rent you a pistol and teach you how to shoot. Buying a modern weapon requires advice they can provide."

The car doors slammed. As he pulled away, I thanked him for his help.

The tune ran through my head again as I headed back across the road to catch a streetcar downtown to meet Red and Will at the Metropole. It had been a long day. Where did they get their dollars? I had an inclination to knock on Mr. O's door for a little tête-à-tête but Mr. O probably knew I was responsible for his two boys undergoing damage control downtown. Red or Will—or better yet both—would have the pleasure of meeting Mr. O.

But as my old man said, "Sufficient unto the day is the evil thereof." I believe my father borrowed the quote from St. Matthew. Standing there waiting, I thought about what Ernie Dalton had said, decided to swing by the Sterling Tower and put the office gun in the bottom drawer where it belonged before heading down to King and York. I swear the holster had worn a patch of skin off of my left side.

METROPOLE SUMMIT NUMBER FOUR—RED'S VERSION

Will and I waited for Al for ages. I worried. Bruno quipped that Al tore out of the Metropole this morning after he took a phone call and did not even notice the blond with a lace collar sitting near the bar. Not like him at all. As it was well past eight, Will and I decided dinner was in order. Will asked for a rye—surprise, surprise—a couple of pickled eggs and sausage with the special frim-fram sauce. John looked puzzled and turned to check the board.

"Don't think we have that . . ." John said tentatively, unsure exactly how he was being set up.

Will laughed, "Don't worry. It's a joke, John. Loosen up. It's a title of a song. You probably heard Bernie play it." He started ta-la-la-ling-ing the tune.

John looked at me as if I were a life boat on the edge of Will's sea. "Ignore him. You should know better by now. Shandy, fish and chips. Rye and the usual pickled stuff for him. Thanks, JT."

We sat a while. I turned and looked straight at Will. "I'm worried about Al. I stopped by the office this afternoon taking care of the bills and checking in with the message service. The daily papers were not there and the office gun was gone, pulled straight out of its box. Why's Al late? Usually he's here first, way before us, scribbling away in his notebook."

"He's a big boy, Rose Red. Al'll be here before you know it." Will said in his lazy tone, but he had been scanning the room and watched as the door opened and shut, opened and shut, opened . . .

As if cued, Al rushed through the Gent's door. Will smiled laconically, caught my eye, then laughed and lowered his head. I could brain the two of them. Besides the dust of crystallized snow on Al's jacket, its left side was notably padded. I was right; he was carrying the office gun. He appeared flushed, chilled and rattled, yet relieved when he spotted us. He plonked down in the chair and released Junction air from his lungs.

"Well, I guess you could say we're in a bit of a pickle," said Al. "But it's nothing we can't eat our way through."

"What happened?" I asked. I offered an opening, though this one not as dramatic. John brought our orders along with a second rye for Al. Thoughtful guy. Al seized the opportunity and ordered the meatloaf, yet again, and a draft beer too. All the gun toting must have made him extra thirsty. Our meals and beverages settled, we leaned in for our fourth summit.

Al recounted his day with Cappie's call to arms and ran through to the tale of his old friends, the Dundas Street store keepers. I did not care for any of the events of the day in between the beginning and the end. As he talked he composed himself; Al soft peddled the trouble with the O brothers, the rise of the Maria Street Dark Boys' Association and his hook up with a bookie pal, Bert D, for his visit to the emergency room. Al's summary completed, I recount my conversation with Sarah and her theory that the source of the money being more important to solving the murder than its destination. Of course, Al sat back, shook his head "no" and immediately put me on locating Junior O's girl and son. The assignments had been handed out for our next round of investigations.

Al raised the question of our joining a gun club as Ernie Dalton suggested learning how to shoot handguns with proficiency before carrying one. At this suggestion, Will jumped up, stretched like a cat and announced, "Back in a minute." Off went Will, presumably to the gentleman's room. I held a dubious reputation as a dead eye shot in the Sydenham High School Rifle Club. I helped win the championship for Sydenham in 1938. Yet, in my book, hand guns were a different thing altogether.

"Do I have to join a gun club, Al?" I grabbed Will's absence as an opportunity to be straight. "Don't get me wrong, I can shoot, but I don't feel right about improving my shot with a hand gun. I feel like I would beg trouble."

"You don't have to join anything, Red. But you might want to think about protecting yourself given the ups and downs in this case. It's a rough one. Tell you what. Take some time and think about it," Al said. He slew me with that particular comment. Delaying a response prolongs the agony of inaction.

When Will arrived back at our usual spot and sat down in his usual chair, Al patted Will's shoulder and took the conversation away. "Who do we need to see as per our usual procedures? Friends. Co-workers. Family. Well, I think it might be time to visit Mr. And Mrs. O."

Will twisted a little in the wood chair and hooked his hands around the rails of the arms. "No can do. Roy made me promise not to visit Mrs. O or to mention she hired us. Said the deal was off if we did. And, besides, I already met her."

Al stares at him in that way he stares only at Will. He

held it for thirty seconds. Will stared back. Al drawled, "You did, did you? And, by the way, how would Roy Smith know we spoke to Mrs. O unless you told Roy Smith?"

"C'mon, Al. C'mon. I told you I met her. Remember. And Roy'd know, he'd know. Somebody'd see us and yap. Roy's not the sharpest tool, but he's still a tool. And Mrs. O. She just wants to know, but doesn't want to know, what happened with Junior." Will waved the smoke of the palour aggrievedly as he spoke and kept his eyes off ours.

"Okay, I see how it'll be. Family. Who is left? Not Mrs. O . . . not Mrs. O. No O brothers, I sent the surviving two to the emergency room today. Not the O brothers. Who does that leave? I know what'll work. You and Red will go see Mr. O." Al shone like he had thrown a winning trump while going solo.

After I spurted my shandy over my plate, I coughed. In a flash, John was there with a gentle slap on my back. "You okay, Red?" He looked at Al and Will with suspicion.

"I'm fine, John. Really, I'm fine. It just went down the wrong pipe," I said hoarsely, and strangely sounded like Will around noon. After a feeble recovery, John was satisfied, turned and waited the table he'd abandoned. I stared at Al.

"Great. Will got drunk with the mother. You beat up Mr. O's two living sons and send us out to interview him about his dead son the following day. From all reports, the O's were all openly sparring with each other—or with Junior—in recent months. Thanks for setting us up for what promises to be a fruitful visit." I regretted the

132

sarcasm but I'm afraid of all those O's, O senior chief among them.

"Let's get one thing straight. I beat his sons before the two of them beat the hell out of me. I was given the chance to beat 'em thanks to my old friend—my old friend from the stockyards, I might add Miss Brophy— Bobby Walker," Al raised his voice, unusually animated. "But you got one thing right. Mr. O won't be wanting to talk to me after the rumble at Vigor Oil. That's why you and Will are going. You can't go on your own, neither can Will. Together you can work it. We need to talk to him about his son straight on." He let that sit there.

"I need another Shandy," I replied, needing to sit a while too. Al waved; John cleared our table and took an order for two doubles and a shandy.

I looked at Will. He looked at me. We both knew we had to visit Mr. O.

"Okay. Tomorrow. Early afternoon," said Will. He nodded to Al. "You'll do back up?"

NOVEMBER 17, 1951
GUNSHOT—AL'S VERSION

I woke early, worked out, showered, shaved and had a quick swim in the Y's pristine pool. Having toweled off, brushed my teeth and combed my hair, I pulled on my new slacks and a fresh shirt. A clean pair of black cotton socks—which I bought in packages of six—appealed to my sense of humour. I never could understand why guys bought various colours and lengths of socks because when one went, you had to throw out the pair. My system only required discarding a sock that had developed a hole because the second sock matched every other one in my drawer. I smiled as I pulled on my black Oxfords; they were Dack's and expensive. The antithesis of the socks but they were easy to shine and wore like iron. Skipping breakfast, I took the College streetcar downtown, transferred south at Bay and jumped off at Richmond. I picked up a paper left on the

Bay streetcar, saving three cents. I rode the elevator up to our office—empty, of course.

The surprise of the day was the Toronto Police report. The Police announced agreement with the findings of the Winnipeg Police and the RCMP. The forces, in their infinite wisdom, concluded that the young man found in a refrigerated freight car succumbed to bullet wounds while hunting on October 30th. He took refuge in the railway car as it was convenient shelter, but help had not arrived in time to save him. I read it, re-read it and read it again. I could have read it a hundred times and still would not have believed it. I'm sure I turned red in the face and my temperature rose several degrees as I mulled over a report insulting the intelligence of anyone with a brain. I felt for the family. They had been through an ordeal and would know this was untrue. This would hurt. Sure the father, Nobby and Izzy were hard cases, but Junior O. Oh! He was a tough boy. He had to be, but hunting birds and animals was not something he did. I was steamed. We had uncovered a mountain of facts that came to nothing. We had nothing that would indicate that Junior O had scratched his finger, let alone prove he had been murdered instead of accidentally shot.

The phone rang, interrupting my fuming thoughts. I picked it up after the third ring and, instead of the "Al Green and Associates" announcement we all agreed on using when answering the telephone, I just growled.

"Al?" A quiet female voice said from the other end of the line.

"Yeah," I agreed.

"It's Pickles," she said. I knew who it was immediately. From the time she was old enough to do day-work,

135

Pickles toiled as an assistant mortician at the local undertaker. As young men with a warped sense of humour and no respect for the feelings of others, we had hung the nickname Pickles on the poor girl. It stuck.

She was frightened, but continued, "Can we get together somewhere private and talk?"

I sensed an unusual tone to her voice. Her suggestion that we meet was certainly agreeable, but even if we found someplace private it would be a mistake. A serious conversation between an obviously concerned woman and a private detective conducted in a private place? Not a good idea. I told her to grab a streetcar downtown to Eaton's Department Store, then to go through the store and exit on Queen where great herds of shoppers trooped from Eaton's to Simpson's and back. After this, she would go through Simpson's to their southeast corner and exit as if headed for the Arcade. I would meet her there. Above all, I told her to stay where there are lots of friendly people and whenever possible, a cop or two.

Realizing she was serious and scared, I dropped the nickname and reverted to her given name, Muriel. Her fear sent a tingling sensation down the back of my neck. Despite Ernie Dalton's advice, after checking to see that the .32 was loaded, I slipped on the shoulder holster and then my windbreaker. I wanted to call Red or Will but given the circumstances, it would be ridiculous for me to telephone either one. Would I announce—for the first time since we started this case—that I was scared? Leaving the office, I slipped into the men's room and settled for a nervous pee.

I quickly covered the distance to the agreed meeting

place where Muriel showed up a few minutes later. She hadn't changed much, but I guess I hadn't either. We crossed Richmond Street and then went south on Yonge Street until we got to Bowle's Lunch.

Bowle's was a large working man's cafeteria, and at this time of day it was packed. We got in the line-up and reached the cashier quite quickly. I ordered for both of us—their beef stew was famous and for a buck you got a big bowl and a thick chunk of bread. It was a hearty lunch. I told the cashier we would both have large glasses of milk to go with the stew. He collected the payment—$2.30—before passing our order on to the serving staff behind the counter. I grabbed a couple of trays and we were seated in a couple of minutes. We sat in the midst of construction workers employed in building the new, much-talked-about Toronto Transportation Commission subway. No threat lingered here. A visibly relaxed Muriel and I made quick work of the stew. We tried to talk but our words were intermixed with the conversations around us. It sounded as if the workmen were shouting at one another, when in fact they had done nothing but raised their voices so they could be heard over the raised voices of others. I suggested we find a quieter place to talk.

We jaywalked across Yonge Street and turned west on Temperance Street. The greatest hardware store was the six-story Aikenhead's on Temperance. You could get anything you wanted in that store and, at this time of day, office workers picked up the bits and pieces they needed to ensuretheir projects back at their new bungalow went ahead smoothly. Up on the fourth floor, we found a convenient spot where we could talk. Muriel didn't have a lot to say but what she did say was a stunner. She began by saying the departed had arrived from Winnipeg in a hand sewn shroud, provided by friends of the family.

"We were told in no uncertain terms that we were not to touch the remains. When the coroner came he ordered the shroud to be removed so he could confirm the findings from Winnipeg— probable hunting accident or an accidental death. We were told that another shroud would be provided by friends of the family and, once again, instructed to do nothing. The friends arrived in the early evening and took charge. They transported the poor boy to the family home and proceeded normally."

Muriel paused and took a deep breath, "I was the only one who was allowed into the room after the coroner had left and then only long enough to ensure things were as they should be. Junior had been shot. Obvious. But he'd been shot twice! The result of your usual hunting accident? Even more strange were the marks on his neck and the bruises on his chest. Junior had been throttled! Working quietly and quickly, I double checked. He had been shot yes, but after some horrid person choked the life out of him. The true cause of death was strangulation. Winnipeg police, local police and the Coroner, were not telling the truth when they said it was 'accidental death.' He was strangled and shot, Al! Junior was murdered!"

With tears in her eyes, Muriel let it all out and looked emotionally drained.

"Can you do something about it, Al? The police coroner mustn't lie about a thing like this."

She sniffled. Rested her head on my shoulder. I did the only thing I could. I put my arms around her and held her for a few minutes. We were interrupted by Hector, one of the store clerks who I had spoken with on a number of occasions to get advice on minor repairs (minor to him, not to me) on things for the office.

I hesitated, but Muriel got me off the hook, "I have to get back. I think I've told you what I had to. I'll go now. I feel better having someone listen. I couldn't talk to anyone although I may have mentioned it to Corrie when we had tea together the next morning. But it was eating me up because it is wrong. I know it's wrong. Call me if you need anything or if you think I left something out and you want to go over it again."

At this point, the elevator arrived. Muriel nimbly stepped in, turned, and as the door closed, she smiled. I felt better when I saw her smile.

I turned to Hector who was standing next to the counter where they sold replicas of handguns. They were realistic replicas and from time to time you would read about an attempted hold-up where the perpetrator had been found to have only a "replica" when apprehended. The size, weight, colour, even the smell were all like the real thing.

"I know you know about these things being a private eye and all," he started. "What you probably never thought about is, from time to time, people bring a replica back. The novelty wears off and they don't like having it around the house, and of course, when they try peddling it to a friend or relative, the friend gets suspicious. You know, 'What's wrong with it? Is it stolen? Did you shoot somebody with it?' We take reps back on consignment, offering it for half of the price of a new one. If we sell it, which is rare, we keep twenty percent and give the owner the eighty percent."

Hector paused with eyebrows raised. Perhaps he was waiting for me to acknowledge I understood. I was tempted to say something sarcastic but better judgement dictated that I keep my mouth shut. I nodded agreement.

"Well, recently the boss and I were checking our inventory—we do frequently because people either steal or try to steal the replicas and a couple of times we've caught employees trying to steal them. But they're heavy and hard to conceal. Well, you know that. We have a store policy where employees can borrow one for a very modest fee but with a hefty deposit ensuring its return. This seems to be working out. But, when we checked the inventory yesterday, we found we had one more than we should have had. And guess what, it isn't a replica."

"What is it?" I asked.

"A handgun," he said.

"What kind of handgun?" I said somewhat exasperated. "You know, make, model, calibre."

"Well," he said, "It's a Colt Police Positive, .32 calibre, 2.5 inch barrel. Doesn't seem to have been used much."

"Okay. What's your problem?" I said, being rather obvious.

"We don't sell real handguns. If the police find this in the store, we'll be in all kinds of trouble. On the third floor we sell a lot of hunting rifles, shotguns, hunting paraphernalia and ammunition. But if we're found with a real handgun, we'd lose our license and our jobs. You're a private eye, you got a license and all. We hoped you'd take it off our hands. We'd be grateful," he said, smiling.

"Wrap it up. I'll take it. I'll check it out though, and if I find anything wrong, I'll be back. Let's keep this between us, right?" I said, doing my best imitation of Humphrey Bogart.

He reached under the counter and produced an oddly shaped package wrapped in brown paper and tied with twine. It wasn't too heavy, but it was awkward. Smiling warmly, Hector was obviously relieved. I nodded and headed for the stairs, not risking the elevator. It got crowded and I was starting to smell like a handgun. I headed back to Sterling Tower a couple of blocks away. Taking the narrow staircase up the tower, I finally unlocked our front door, unloaded the Iver Johnson and dropped it back in the bottom drawer. I loaded the Colt and stuck it in the shoulder holster. It felt different but not uncomfortable. It was only a six shot revolver but was a double action, which had added to the size and weight.

I headed for the Metropole and as I did, the familiar lyric filled my thoughts. I knew that around the hotel and in the West Toronto Junction we could put our collective finger on drifters, commuters, con men, crapshooters, and a good number of them would be wearing fancy shirts and collars whenever appropriate. That left me with the rest . . . where did they get their dollars, and what was their Ace in the Hole? I felt like we were close to knowing about the money. My old man used to say, "It's all about money." I knew the way to a solution was to follow the cash flow.

I'M HERE IF YOU NEED ME—AL'S VERSION

Red and Will were going to drop in on Mr. O uninvited, and I suspect, unwelcome. While they were going about our business, I had made it my business to be in the area, so that if things started to go wrong I would be there to help.

Before leaving the office I strapped on the shoulder holster and made sure the new office gun was loaded. Having done that, I slipped on my navy blue waterproof windbreaker, pocketed a handful of purple TTC adult tickets and headed north, around the east side of City Hall, to catch the Dundas streetcar in front of Eaton's Annex. If you ride the same route often enough, you'll find that you have memorized the names of the streets where there are streetcar stops. I got off at Keele Street and started walking west on the north side of Dundas Street.

It was mid-afternoon as I strolled along, furtively looking up ahead, hoping I would not run into Ernie Dalton. I had traded the Iver Johnson for the Colt Police Positive but I hadn't joined a pistol shooting club yet. I had looked at a number of advertisements which suggested that new members were welcome and a couple that offered a free group familiarization session for those of us who knew nothing about pistols and pistol shooting, so the eventual decision to join or not to join would be based on some, albeit limited, knowledge of the activity. I had been put off when I called these pistol clubs, and was cordially informed that a substantial 'good faith' deposit of twenty-five dollars would be required from each of us. If we decided to join, the deposit would be treated as a down payment on our first quarterly membership fee which ranged from one hundred dollars to three hundred dollars depending on the variety of services available. The cost of ammunition was extra. If we decided not to join, our good faith deposit would be partially refunded, as every pistol club contacted charged an administration fee. So the good faith crap was a figment of somebody's imagination and my enthusiasm for this particular endeavour evaporated rather rapidly.

I suddenly realized why so many bank tellers were being held up at gunpoint. These robbers were undoubtedly pistol club members who needed the cash to pay the cost of their membership. Another good example of something sounding better than it really is.

I slipped into a bit of nostalgia when I passed the Beaver Theatre and wondered if Mr. Murphy was still the manager. I had worked there as an usher when I was a student at Western Tech. The theory was that by working three or four nights a week, I could afford to start dating some lucky girl. Practically speaking, working three or four nights a week didn't leave enough free time to date a girl, until school closed for the summer at which point a lot of the better-off girls left town with their parents to enjoy life at their summer cottage. Looking up at the marquee, I noted that the feature presentation was The Great Caruso which starred Mario Lanza. The name of the second feature sent a shiver down my spine—The Double Deal—which starred Marie Windsor. My concern for my two associates grew.

A little further down the street I saw David Turner in front of the Liberty Dance Hall. He was obviously preparing the premises for a wedding reception. It was then that I noticed that the block between Pacific Avenue and High Park Avenue was longer than the usual Junction block. I assumed this was the result of using the straightaways of the long gone Carleton Racetrack as the more southerly end of these parallel streets. I felt some pride in knowing that Sir Casimir Gzowski found the time in what must have been a hectic life in the mid-1800s and, considering his many accomplishments, was involved in the inaugural running of the Queen's Plate at West Toronto Junction's Carleton Raceway in 1860.

As I neared Quebec Avenue, I smiled in anticipation of running into Joe Indovina whose family had been selling my dear mother fresh fruits and green groceries for years. It was a Saturday, and the Indovina family were busy with their numerous customers who, having received their weekly wages, were stocking up for the weekend. "Another time," I thought.

As I passed the Purity Dairy, I was tempted to drop in for one of their legendary "three glasses for a nickel" milkshakes, but like all working men of our era, taking a break was something my employer did not permit. A little further along, I noticed Jimmie's Tire Shop was still in business. During World War II, the manufacturers stopped making automobile tires altogether for the civilian market. The shortage of road rubber, coupled with the rationing of gasoline, became so acute that some owners just put their autos up on concrete blocks and left them up for the war's duration. Jimmie's was an astounding enterprise. A very small shop, they produced retreads for a hungry market. As soon as it became apparent that the war was going to end, the manufacturers started pouring much sought-after tires into the willing market. Jimmie's business skidded to a halt and would have gone flat if he hadn't smartly concentrated on retreading specialty tires. The large manufacturers wouldn't bother with retreading because of the low volume of business for that class of tire.

Further on, I felt a chuckle as I caught sight of the Maltese community's church which was still only a large basement. The people of the congregation, mindful of the destruction of their homeland during World War II, were quite content to see what money they could spare in restoring their homeland. Someday, I thought, they will build a beautiful church that will be practical, in addition to its beauty and its adherence to the tradition of the Maltese people.

To my surprise, Paul Seberras and Nathan Starr were standing in front of the church discussing something. Although we went to different high schools, I would frequently walk part of the way home with Paul and Nate, both of whom attended Humberside Collegiate. Nate had just come from the Junction Shul, and as we stood cheerfully amidst a long catch-up conversation, that damn song started running through my head, louder than usual . . . . They all had that ace down in the hole! Then it clicked. A Jew, a Maltese Catholic and an Anglican cheerfully reminisce about their schooldays. I was the Anglican, of course, and before my voice changed as a boy, my mother had enrolled me as a member of the choir at the Church of the Advent on Pritchard Avenue. We had quite a number of boys in the choir at that time and I thought we added a touch of class that would otherwise be absent. One of the boys in the choir had eventually become a jockey, initially working thorough-breds and eventually riding at the local racetracks. He was one of the several jockeys who had been set down that summer for allegedly fixing races and I was quite positive he could, if he was so inclined, shed some light on the situation involving the murder of Junior O. As the reunion with Paul and Nate ended, I resolved to call and test the waters with another old associate who could set me on the right track to the solution of Junior's murder.

Back at the Double R, I looked up the telephone number in the white pages and dialed it. A raspy, mature female voice answered after the sixth ring, and when I asked to speak with John, she quickly told me that I had the wrong number and just as quickly hung up. I would have to plan my next move with a little more care.

As I was here because of my concern for Red and Will, I strolled east on the south side of Dundas. Crossing Gilmour, I wondered if the doors to the Garlic were open. When I got there, I found that they were. I went in and stood in the lobby concealed by the double glass doors. Harry, the usher, soon materialized and advised it was too early for admission to the evening performance.

"I'm keeping my eye on things, Harry." I said.

He stood beside me for a minute or so, peering across at the building where two-thirds of Green & Associates were now in session.

"I saw them when they arrived and watched them walk in like they belonged," he said quietly. "I knew you'd be around somewhere and people would be looking over their shoulders. It probably doesn't matter. A buck short and a day late."

I asked if I could use the office telephone and—only because no one else was around—the phone was free and completely private as Harry went about his business. I called Freeman's Pool Hall and luckily caught up with Cappie—he was a spectator as a result of the lack of the necessary bread. He agreed to round up as many of the

Maria Street Dark Boy's Association as he could on short notice and set them about locating the missing jockey. Cappie and I would meet for breakfast at the Double R on Monday to discuss results.

When they came out, we would head for the Metropole and slake the thirst we would develop thinking about what we would slake our thirst with when we got to the Metropole. Life's like that.

IF I KNEW YOU WERE COMING I'D'VE BAKED A CAKE— RED'S VERSION

I dressed in a cable knit sweater, slacks and boots today as the temperature was losing the struggle with the freezing point. Last night's snow provided ornamentation for the 38th Annual Eaton's Santa Claus Parade.

Upon exit from my apartment, I banged on Pam Esson's door while holding a bag of frozen peas and corn, a bottle of milk, butter and half a dozen eggs. I started the laborious task of defrosting the freezer: I propped the fridge door open, wiped the fridge clean, stuck baking trays on the racks under the freezer, and blanketed the area in front with towels. In a strange way, I enjoyed defrosting the fridge having grown up using an ice box. The door opened, Pam took the groceries saying, "Why in heaven's name do you defrost your fridge once a month? Never mind, let's get together for tea Sunday." We had not seen each other in a while, but I agreed and hoped she would not start in about her missing father. Down the switchback stairs and out, Will and I met earlier than normal, in anticipation of the traffic with suburban parade goers, costumed participants of all ages and frustrated drivers boxed by the Dupont and University road closures.

Before I met Will, I stopped in the corner store at the top of Huron to borrow their telephone. The clerk doesn't mind lending if you're one of her regulars. I dialed the number after thanking Kate; Sarah picked up the line after the third ring.

"Dotty, we gotta keep this short. Not the best day for you to be calling me," she said after our hellos.

"Thanks, Sarah. I figured you wouldn't mind," I replied.

"I don't, but my mother minds. If she does, I mind too. Keep it short."

After a deep breath, I said, "I need to talk with Junior's girlfriend."

"What's that got to do with me?" Sarah's tone was flat.

"Might you help? Somebody on Maria must know how to reach her. It's just that I have no idea where to start looking for her in Corktown, really I don't. To tell you the truth, I don't even think I've set foot east of Yonge except for the time Al took me to hear Louis Armstrong play. I don't know the girlfriend's name but she might know something that will break this case. We're getting close but, truthfully, we're stuck." I'd spoken too fast again.

"That's one lame detective firm you're working with Dots."

"Sarah, please."

"Just for you. Understand. Just for you. I'll give it a shot." With this, Sarah banged down the handset. I thanked the young clerk and Kate replied simply, "Later gator." The doorbell jangled as I walked out the door.

A first-time occurrence: Will was standing at the corner waiting for me. The streetcar boarded a minute later—we grabbed a transfer in order to jump off and catch the Dundas car. Travel was slow going west with the heavy automobile traffic and Will picked up an Eaton's Santa Claus Parade Colouring Book which had fallen beside an empty seat. Thumbing through the copy, Will proclaims a sense of kinship with Punkinhead based on the redemptive story of his hair, but he expresses disappointment at the comic's inclusion of a Robinson Crusoe float. Will said Crusoe cultivated an island only to make it a British colony.

"Will. They're not real. They are put in the parade and in a colouring book for kids. It's just for fun," I pointed out.

"Put in the parade for kids and their families for fun and to encourage spending money, you mean. Where is Santa going? Toyland at Eaton's, right? Characters themselves may not be real, but they represent real things," he countered.

"Don't start." I was anxious about our trip upstairs from the barrel shop to Mr. O's bookie office. My nervousness was probably why Will talked about the parade's participants in the first place.

"Notice how there's no float for Jurgis and Ona." Will passed the do-not-start point.

"I'll bite. Who's Jurgis and Ona?"

"You still haven't read The Jungle yet, have you RB? Why do you disappoint me so much?"

"Because I can. What about putting them in the Labour Day Parade? If I read it, will you promise never mentioning that bloody book again?"

"Never's a really really long time, RB."

"Yes or no on the book, Will." I said.

"Maybe," he replied.

Will's words distract me from the task ahead. Sadly, we reached the end of the line mid-afternoon. We walked along the diagonal towards the barrel factory west of Gilmore. I peeked in the window of the Double R to see if Al was shooting the breeze with one of his pals. The Double R would be a great spot to back us up. He was not there but he would be around Dundas somewhere packing. I considered leaving a message for Al with George, but decided we would see Al later at the Metropole. Will and I picked the south side for our approach to Mr. O's office because of his third storey windows. We stood and talked for five minutes across from the store as we wanted to give the street a good view of us too.

"Ready, Red?" said Will.

"No, but don't tell Al. Let's get this over with," I replied as we dodged traffic crossing Dundas. In front of the nondescript building, steel drums were scattered at random on the sidewalk. We entered through a plain brown door. Once through, we started the ascent up the narrow staircase with dirt tracked on the walls and treads marking years of heavy use. On the third floor landing, dust settled in the half moon impressions on the trim and door—indentations from police sledgehammers, was my guess. Pausing at the top, we heard mumbled voices from within. Will took a deep breath and rapped hard three times. Silence.

"Hello," Will projected his voice towards the door. "Is

Mr. O in the office? We'd like a word with him . . . if we may."

Will was always well-spoken. The silence was broken by the sound of a chair being pushed back, followed by heavy footsteps tramping across the wooden floor. The door swung away from us quickly, revealing what I believed was the face of Mr. O: an imposing man who stood over six feet tall with a beefy, but not paunchy, build. He wore grey trousers and a white shirt with rolled up sleeves over a cotton t-shirt. His small eyes were set in a broad face surrounded by wide frays of thinning hair. His expression conveyed wrath and his stance, power. Framed by the door, he stood motionless and silent.

Behind him, the room's sole illumination was the sunlight peeking between the slats and ribbons of the venetian blinds. Boards chalked with racetracks and horses were tacked up on the south wall, scraps of paper spilled out of the garbage cans and water topped up a couple of buckets on the floor. Two switchboards lined the north wall. Along with a telegraph, a few dozen black phones sat on scattered tables. Four cases of Seagram's were stacked between two windows by a radiator. This was what looked to be the biggest back-end in the Junction. After fishing around in his jacket pocket, Will extended his hand with a business card; I offered mine too. But Mr. O remained immobile. "Mr. O, I presume. I'm Dorothy Brophy and this is Will Jones. We work with Al Green and have been hired to investigate the murder of your son, Junior. First, let us say, our deepest condolences for your loss."

Still nothing from Mr. O, but I heard someone inside

the room.

Will said, "If you have a moment, we'd like to speak to you about Junior."

"If I knew you were coming, I'd've baked a cake," Mr. O replied.

Awkward was the most charitable word for this interview.

I tried a question next: "If I may, when did you first notice Junior was missing?"

"Don't have to tell you nothing," he replied. For a fleeting moment, I feared Will would correct his grammar.

Will said instead, "You're right. You don't. But the thing is, we're hired and we're investigating. A murder's a murder, right? Don't you want to know what happened?"

"Know what happened? I'll tell you what happened. Police shot him and threw him in a boxcar westward bound. This city treats us worse than animals. And now, today in the paper, the police cover it up with a verdict of accidental death."

"Well," said Will. "The police theory is one we've virtually ruled out."

Mr. O exploded, "Of course you'd rule it out! Huge surprise from you Greens and Jones."

"I'm a Brophy," I replied.

"Same thing," he growled. "Now get out of my property. No more questions from the likes of you!"

"We're going, going . . . we'll leave." I replied, putting up both hands with my palms facing towards him. I felt an odd compulsion to provoke during the dud of an interview. "One thing before we go. If you got the police pegged as the killers, what was the point of Izzy and Norbert waiting at Vigor Oil yesterday to beat up our associate, Al?"

"Thanks to your associate, my boys end up in the emergency room. He's the brute. Good thing he didn't have a gun or they'd both be dead too. Get out, get out!"

"We're going, we're going," I replied and half turned.

Will said, "Oh, just one last thing, really this time. Al asked me to give you something." He handed over the straight razor Al picked up off the Vigor Oil floor. Mr. O looked confused.

Just then, past Mr. O's shoulder, I glimpsed a young man with a bruise on the side of his face standing by a desk. As he looked like a member of the O family and, since his arm was in a sling, my guess was he was Izzy. Whoever he was, he smiled, looking straight at me. He reached one hand to lift the sling and slipped the other inside as if to pull a gun from a holster. Smiling, he slowly drew his hand out. In a flash, his hand extended with his index finger pointed towards me. His thumb raised like the hammer on a revolver. He narrowed one eye and squeezed the trigger with his third finger like he was shooting a pistol.

"Pow," he exhaled from his lungs.

Straight to my gut, that warning shot.

METROPOLE SUMMIT NUMBER FIVE—RED'S VERSION

Leaving Mr. O's bookmaking office, Will and I walked down the stairs between the third and second floors, but raced down the final set. Well, I raced down the final set. Once out the door, I dodged automobiles crossing Dundas in the hope of catching a downtown streetcar immediately. Will knew how to take care of himself.

"Whoa there, Red!" I heard someone yelling.

I looked, and there, looking puzzled, was Al standing beside a young usher in front of the Crescent Theatre.

"Everything okay, Will?" Al cocked his head a bit and yelled as Will appeared from the side door of the barrel factory with a cigarette already lit.

I heard nothing in reply. A hand gesture, I presumed, was offered and received. Al approached me when I was safely on the sidewalk. He reached out, "Wanna go over to the Double R for a tea? You okay?"

"No to tea in that dive and no to being okay. I'll take the streetcar downtown like we agreed last night. Oh look, there's one turning out of the loop now. I think I can catch it."

I said goodbye, and sprinted the two blocks towards the streetcar stop, barely making it in time to board the car. Alpine slacks and rubber boots were a smart wardrobe choice today. My associates would catch up for grub and suds or, more accurately, grubs and spirits in quick time. Who cared about appearances at this point? The O's surely saw my speedy crossing of Dundas. Al and Will would repair any non-private-eye-like appearances on the street and those caused by my exit in a wild style. Safely seated in the middle section of the streetcar, I caught a glimpse of my associates in front of the Crescent or the Chive, or whatever it is Al calls the movie theatre. They posed with a tough guy demeanour for the street and for the third floor.

The downtown traffic was abysmal as the streetcar crawled along Dundas with a jerky stop-and-go motion. By the time we reached Bloor, standing room was only available inside, and by Bathurst, the car was so packed, no one could board. The streetcars were delayed by the automobile traffic on Toronto's terminally congested streets. The usual late afternoon Saturday rush of shoppers joined the thousands of Santa Claus Parade participants and 700,000 watchers who zigzagged home from the parade. Added to this seasonal mix was the opening of the Royal Agricultural Winter Fair, where horse show riders and watchers oozed well-heeled respectability. Tomorrow, the city would be shut tight and the Dundas car from Runnymede to city hall would take less than the posted 27 minutes. Anything less than that doesn't matter because on Sundays, there was nothing to do.

Reaching the Metropole's Ladies' Entrance, I pondered what my answer should be to the inevitable "what happened" question. I'll just tell the truth. Izzy scared me. Nothing wrong with that answer. As I walked in, I noted Bruno waiting for my return. Arms straight with his hands planted on the bar, his head was tilted back. He nodded me over.

"You okay?" he asked.

"Yeah, I'm okay."

Pause.

"Al left a telephone message for you that he and Will will be here soon."

"I know they will."

"That's a rough business you're in. You should take care of yourself and find a better job. Life is short, you know."

"I know and I will. I'm thinking of going back home soon."

I headed to our table. The band was playing Mood

Indigo with a melancholic zeal. Once seated, some soldier asked if he could join me. I definitely refused the request warning, I hoped, all the other guys in the parlour. Al and Will showed up an hour later, engaged in their usual banter about this and that, like where Boyd and the Jacksons might be holed up and the possibility of a Leaf win in Chicago tonight. No one mentioned my quick departure from Mr. O's office, of course.

Although evasive about who, where and how, Al came into possession of a new gun and ruled out pistol training as yet another crooked racket. Tomorrow, I thought I'd talk to my friend, Pam Esson. Pam knew something about shooting a pistol. When bank robberies increased after the war, the banks offered pistol shooting courses to their tellers and managers. Pam enrolled in the course and loved shooting at the range.

Our summit continued much as it always did, with familiar food and drink. We learned a few new things today. The Enforcement forces—and, by extension, the newspapers—were supporting the original western ruling of accidental firearm death. Izzy and Mr. O asserted that the police were covering up Junior's murder, while Mrs. O feared but desired anyways to learn the name of the murderer. One of Al's old school friends collaborated with Kat's assertion that Junior was strangled or throttled. Izzy's fake pistol gesture was chalked up to posturing, but then again Al and Will did not see Izzy's routine. Al said he was nervous. I said I was scared of the O's. Mr. O and Izzy did not want us on this case.

Will said he's gonna hit the Colonial with some friends.

NOVEMBER 18, 1951
IT IS SUNDAY . . . YAWN!—AL'S VERSION

Trying to find something to do on a Sunday in Toronto could be a problem. No, let me correct that. Trying to find something to do on a Sunday in Toronto was a problem, but as the years passed, some progress was made toward the removal of typical Sunday restrictions. But it was a slow progress.

In the winter months, when those of us who went were not at church, we could take advantage of the natural ice that the good Lord provided and indulge in a game of shinny that lasted as long as there were two willing skaters. This only applied to those days when it hadn't snowed, as the scrapers and shovels were locked away on Sundays.

When we were young, our summer was filled with activities at the local playground by the local public school or park. Ours boasted one female supervisor and one male supervisor. It had big swings, small or baby swings, a sandbox complete with pails and shovels, a teeter-totter, a tether pole, a softball field complete with wire screen, a bag full of bases, bats and balls—some of which were still in usable condition—and a volleyball net sometimes made valuable by the existence of a volleyball. This ball however was often too soft to use and if you could locate a needle valve to inflate the ball, you would be lucky to find a pump that it fit that actually worked. This didn't apply to Sunday when the playground was locked up as tight as a drum, just like it was at sundown on weekdays. If Jesus really loved the little children, don't you think he would have allowed them the facilities to recreate their little bodies on Sundays?

That Sunday, after a quick swim, shower and shave, I dressed casually and attended the lunch counter where I was served overcooked bacon and eggs, dried out toast with a little butter and a mug of lukewarm rancid coffee, unimproved by the addition of milk. I leafed through the copies of the week's newspapers that were stacked on the end of the counter. The Canadian dollar was still accepted at par or above by the Buffalo and Rochester, New York retailers who I was sure would be open to serve their Canadian customers. Our retail stores were locked up tight and, while no one begrudged them a day off, those that provided necessities could have stayed open on a rotating basis. The gas stations did that. A group of them would work together with one open and the others remaining closed on Sunday. A different station remained open each Sunday. Even with that, the car owners tried to ensure that their tanks were full on Saturday to avoid running around looking for the station that was open. This was particularly ludicrous during World War II when gasoline—and other things (meat, butter, sugar, beer)—were rationed.

Automobile tires were not rationed but new ones were not rolling off the production line and as tires wore down, car owners scrambled for replacements. Retreads were not very satisfactory. Some owners just put their cars up on blocks and left them there for the duration.

Our alarm clock stopped working in those days; my family was in a bind for a long while. Fortunately, my father worked nights so he would wake the rest of the family in the morning and rely on us to wake him in the late afternoon. One day as we neared the end of hostilities, I was walking past Woolworth's or Kresge's, I can't remember which, but I saw a window display of Westclox alarm clocks. I quickly went in and purchased a clock so badly needed by the family. I think they sold out the entire shipment in a few hours that day.

In the several years following the shortages of World War II, Toronto was ready for anything alleged to be entertainment. With men away serving our country, women helped fill the gap, doing what were traditionally regarded as men's jobs, and doing them very well. They earned good pay cheques and put the money into war savings bonds, partly because consumer goods were not being produced. Once the men returned from the war, the women gave up their jobs. A new industrial demographic was created: The Baby Boom.

Sunday sports legislation, when it finally came, was a mixed blessing. It allowed teams such as Toronto's baseball Leafs to play on Sundays, but it also dictated that they had to observe a 6 p.m. curfew. Their season was long over of course, and the hockey Leafs didn't bother scheduling Sunday afternoon games (in part given the circumstances) and since they regularly played at home on Saturday night. But still, Maple Leaf Gardens' management never missed a chance to make a dollar. On Thursday nights, they regularly presented a professional wrestling program frequently headlined by Toronto's hero: Whipper Billy Watson. They arranged for the senior amateur Toronto Marlboroughs to play Friday nights and the Juniors to present a double header on Sunday afternoons—all games to capacity crowds. Senior commercial leagues played Wednesday and Friday nights at Varsity Arena and Ravina Gardens with substantial fan support.

In the years following the shortages of World War II, Toronto was ready for anything that smacked of entertainment. They had trouble finding it on Sunday. The population listened to the comedic and drama radio programs broadcasted from or through Buffalo, New York, which, thanks to modern technology, the working man could be received on a radio without an antenna. The federal government had discontinued the requirement to pay an annual license fee if you owned a radio receiver.

I didn't spend a lot of time going over the week's newspapers that morning, as I had read at least one every day that week. I went for a walk and eventually grabbed a streetcar and headed home to visit the folks. They were always as glad to see me as I was glad to see them. They were interested in my business (as they called it) and wondered if it was a success. The truth was, they preferred if I gave up this private detective thing and got a nice, reliable job clerking—they pronounced it "clarking"—in one of the proliferation of banks that existed. They existed as mechanization, as another casualty of the European hostilities—now all the accounts were handwritten.

One thing about being at home on a Sunday afternoon was my mother's cooking. I really loved a home cooked meal. She served up the usual roast beef that my father carved with roast potatoes, Yorkshire pudding, brussel sprouts and carrots—all floating in pan gravy. I had seconds of everything and vowed that I would have to come home on Sunday afternoons more often.

I didn't stay too late as I knew we had a busy day on Monday. I didn't go directly back to the Y either. I went downtown to The Sterling Tower and picked up the new office cannon. I expected we might be faced with a showdown shortly and I was determined to be ready.

AIM FOR THE BLUR—RED'S VERSION

After I retrieved my food and placed it in my clean fridge, I headed back down the hall for tea and scones with Pam. Pam and I took the school bus together in Tweed and shot in the rifle club in high school. We had good times together. I remember one fall day during the war, we had hiked out of town and shot at a flock of ducks. At first we couldn't figure out what was happening, we thought it was hailing. We then realized the pellets were falling down around us; "Incoming!" Pam yelled between whoops. A tender amazon, she had a propensity for dreaming and directness. As I left my apartment, I double-checked the lock on my door. The twins across the hall were at it again about some foul play regarding shoes. What a duo.

Pam's door was still open.

"Robbers, killers, thieves, walk right into Pam's apartment, take and do whatever you want please," I yelled as I swung in the door.

"Dottsy, really. You act like Moll Flanders lives down the hall," Pam replied as she sets the Brown Betty teapot down on the table beside the plate of scones.

"She'd be a welcome change from the two dirty blonds across from my place, I swear."

"Please don't swear."

We sat at the yellow laminate table with matching yellow chairs. Pam avoided talk about her family and instead shared the gossip among tellers about the two-week-old Don Jail Prison breakout by three bank robbers. While Pam aced the pistol course offered by the Bank of Toronto last year, she worried about her fellow tellers and, more particularly, her manager having access to pistols in the event of a robbery.

"Honestly Dottsy, it's not rocket science," Pam puffed. "Half of them couldn't hit a target by the end of the course and my manager is the worst. Being kind, Mr. Sean is near sighted and needs new glasses. He hit my target more than once."

"That's bad. Of course, you're always pretty sharp with a rifle. But what'd you say the difference is between firing a rifle and a pistol?"

"No doubt, pistols are trickier. You can support a rifle against your arm if you have to from a standing position and the trajectory is predictable once you get the feel of the rifle. Shotguns go wide. But you need steadiness and focus with a pistol. Pistols hit targets only when held with two hands, arms out, elbows locked with feet spread and knees locked. If you don't focus and hold steady before you shoot, the bullet will end up wide, or either in somebody else or ricocheting off, I dunno, a bank vault door. I tell you, it's scary the banks offered the training." Pam shook her head.

"Scary, especially if someone's pointing a rifle at you in a bank full of people," I replied. "Any other difference between a pistol and a rifle?"

"Well, the sight, I suppose. The bullet follows the eye, as they say. I focus on the target and aim for the centre. Our instructor says, if your target is moving, 'Focus on the blur.' This means keep your eye on the target, like with rifle shooting, but focus on the target's movements using the pistol's sight. Pistols have a little barrel. Look at the blur with the best eye, squeeze smoothly on the trigger, breathe slowly and hold the pistol tight" Pam pauses, looking dead at me.

"You in trouble, Dots?"

"Nay, it's just the case we're on has me a bit spooked. One of our suspects pantomimed shooting me yesterday," I said. She looked at me for a while without speaking.

"You really should practice with a pistol before firing it. They're harder than one might think. Want the name of the range the banks use?"

"Sure, but later, may I? I think I'm going over to St. Cecilia's to sit a spell. I miss that place."

163

NOVEMBER 19, 1951
IT SEEMS I'VE HEARD THAT SONG BEFORE—AL'S VERSION

This morning I realized, with some surprise, that I was singing in the shower. I was singing Ace In The Hole and I knew then that we were on the right track.

Will and I had unknowingly taken a great leap forward when we faced the simple fact that it was virtually impossible for one jockey to fix a horse race, other than the rather obvious situation where the odds-on favourite is held up by the jockey and others allowed to pass. It would take several jockeys to agree to the desired finish. What stuck out in my mind was the fact that in the summer of last year, two jockeys had been handed 50 day suspensions by the Ontario Racing Commission for "unsatisfactory riding and reprehensible conduct"— whatever the hell that is—and a third jockey was given a lesser sentence for "unsatisfactory riding."—How can you tell when it's unsatisfactory? I don't bet on a horse very often, but every time I do and he doesn't win, I swear it was due to "unsatisfactory riding."

Then, quite recently, at the end of October to be exact, a jockey named Robert Wankmueller testified in court to distributing sums of money to a large number of jockeys, who in exchange agreed to ensure that their mounts would not finish first or second. A bookmaker named Harry Schwartz and his wife, Ann, allegedly masterminded and bankrolled the fix. Wankmueller was on the favourite, who seemed to be boxed in in the early going, and in the backstretch should have fired and closed with the leaders but just didn't. I think he finished last.

The way Will and I figured it, an unknown person(s) had tipped off Junior O to the name of the probable winner and his fortune was then made. Yet, exactly how his fortune was made was a mystery. Our initial reaction was that he had made a large wager with his old man using an assumed name but that didn't wash. If you place a bet with a bookie, any bookie, you get paid off as soon as the results are official. Junior's money was being delivered in packets, twice a week. Figure that one out.

So that is what I set out to do that morning; as I sang in the shower. Junior got his dollars because he had an ace-in-the-hole. Actually more than one. No one bookmaker in the city could have taken the financial hit that would result in a payoff as large as that which was gradually dribbling into Junior's hands. Well, his old man could have, but if the bet had been made with Mr. O, the result would be well-known in and beyond the

West Toronto Junction area. I headed for the Double R.

It was early in the day and George was busy preparing for the customers who would start showing up soon. Thankfully, he had a pot of freshly-made coffee ready, so we sat down and had a cup. I told him that I expected Cappie and he didn't budge.

"Cappie will be in for his morning coffee sometime after 10. If he doesn't show by noon, he has gone directly to the Alps Restaurant for lunch. Kat and Nakev will not be in for the usual pick-up because it's not one of the designated days and she no longer uses Nakev as an escort as she figures she is tougher than he is anyway."

I was gob-smacked! Junior O was long gone, and the money that was supposedly coming from him was still flowing.

I couldn't figure out why the money was still flowing, although I immediately suspected Mrs. O, but I wanted to talk to the jockey that Junior had some arrangement with. Cappie came through the door. Looking like he had been up all night, he plonked himself down in the booth and gulped the hot coffee that George had poured for him.

"No luck with the jockey," he said without surprising me. "But I talked with his old man who will not join us but is waiting in front of the hardware store. He's on his way to work."

"Did the old man say anything that might interest us?" This could be classed as a stupid question, but what the hell.

"No," he said very flatly.

"I'll go talk with him then." I said getting up to leave and noticing that Cappie was as exhausted as anyone could be.

"Thanks Cappie," I said as I started to leave, "and thank the others who helped. We'll get even when this mess is cleared up."

"There were no others," he said without a smile. "Kat put the word out that she knew the answers and would take care of it and that there was no need to bother anyone anymore."

"What in the name of hell is going on?" I said. More to myself than anyone else. Kat was getting to be a pain in the ass. We'd have to talk this out.

BLACK CATS CREEP ACROSS MY PATH—RED'S VERSION

Sarah Pope delivered again. She organized a meeting with Junior's girlfriend, Crissie.

We met Crissie at the lunch counter in Simpson's basement shortly after noon. The silver counter was lined with shoppers and business folk dressed mostly in black and seated on red vinyl swivel stools. Petite and freckled, Crissie's most arresting features were her bold, blue eyes and cheshire smile. After introductions and reassurances, Sarah took her leave.

"What can you tell me about the last time you heard from Junior?" I asked Crissie.

"Well, Junior started his collections earlier than usual because the sun starts setting 'round five now. He works at night mostly. After the last collection, Junior was thinking about seeing Francis Goes to the Races at the Beaver just for a laugh, he said. He was enjoying his last month in the Junction, especially when he heard the forecast of that big storm. Junior said a snow storm in early November signals a long winter. But he liked the snow, a soft blanket that covers the crap and dulls the noise, he'd say. But in the Junction, the soot starts laying over everything in a day or two."

"It was going to be his last winter here? Why? Where was he going?" I asked.

Voice unsteady, Crissie continued, "Well, Junior, baby Josh and I were all going to Florida. Junior got us tickets on the New Royal Palm direct to Miami. A fresh start, Junior said. But not anymore." Crissie teared up and I handed her my handkerchief.

"You can keep it. I'm sorry for your loss," I added. She started, "I could go with Josh, but the two of us on our own?"

"I know, travelling with a baby alone would be hard. But why Florida?" I coached.

"Junior knew people who knew people down there. Junior's plan—until the day we were set to leave on December 13th—was keeping up his collections, thus keeping the old man from getting up his nose any more than he usually does. Though his parents pretend like they don't know the outside world, his father will always be pissed about my getting in the family way. Pissed is sorta his old man's normal state, but what jazzes me more is his father acts like he's a ghost. Like Junior did not exist. Gone. Departed. Vanished. Bah, like his family's the neighbourhood's biggest upstanding citizens and all. My family feels the same, but they can't keep it up. They love baby Josh. His brother Izzy feeds the family fire by asking, right in front of Junior's parents, after Mick-Ress Crissie and her love child, Jolly. Lately, Nobby and Izzy were pointedly asking about his bookie connections and new jockey friends."

"We've heard about the tension between Junior's brothers and father. What ya know?" I asked.

"Well, Junior always had a score to settle with Izzy and Nobby. Nobby's a plodder; Izzy's a schemer. You know the kind—what does this, that and the other thing mean for the long run. Izzy's always looking for the angles. On occasion, Izzy might pound somebody out, but only after he's looked at what might happen as a consequence 10 feet down the road. Junior kept away from him the best he could. Izzy is his father's son and if Mr. O said something, you can bet Izzy said it too. Then there's Mrs. O. She cared for Junior, he was her youngest. But she all but wrote him off until we had Josh. She hinted a few times to Junior she wants to see the baby, but when and where . . . That's the state of Junior's family relations in a nutshell."

Crissie leaned back and dug into her steak and kidney pie in front of her. Fish and chips for me. We ate together in silence as it was the first meal of the day for us both.

Suddenly Crissie stopped and declared, "I say, the hell with the lot of 'em."

Then she gestured, "Pardon my french. But, the hell with 'em. Junior made a will and left everything to me and Josh. If anything happened to us, for some weird reason, he left it to his loser brothers, Izzy and Nobby. Go figure."

An alarm rang in my brain.

"There's only one person in the whole stinking neighbourhood I trust," said Crissie. "Kat, my old school friend, lent me her ear when I was expecting Josh and had a talk with Junior. She dreamed up using the preacher as a go-between. Banking on a mission preacher is weird, but desperate times call for desperate measures. Junior got the money to Kat, Kat to the preacher and Preacher Jack ferried money down Maria Street. No questions asked about the source of his money. They knew better. Kat fixed it with somebody who ferries the funds for "the betterment of the common good," as they say. After all, an innocent baby is involved. Nobody liked it much, but the funds still came to me and Josh. Don't ask, I won't tell you who—and to Junior's bank account for the longer term—for our move to Miami. I figure they thought it was worth the trouble as it meant one less O in the neighbourhood."

"I'm sure that's not true," I interrupted. Crissie sure likes talking. "But getting back to the night in question, can you remember anything he said about the collection?"

"Junior's call on October 30th was on Ryding across the tracks but close to his home. He said he had to see another packing house loser about an unpaid debt and was going to reason with 'im with some hard knuckle sandwiches. He was going to hoof it across the tracks."

Crissie started to reminisce, "Before I had Josh, he showed me the route across the tracks when we went to Ryding Park for a few laughs. We headed along Dundas, up Pacific and over to Vine. North of Roman Meal Company's arch, the fence is torn back as folks from St. Clair cross there for Dundas Street shopping. Once through the fence, we scuttled across 10 train tracks dodging back and forth along, behind, or under the cars like we was kids. Junior said to pay attention to those wrought iron towers lighting the yards and to mind the inspectors and keep low. Once across, we passed the car repair shops and sauntered like we belonged on West Toronto Street and over to Ryding Avenue."

I listened and waited for her to return to the story of Junior's last collection.

"Ryding Park is the best place to watch the trains moving through Toronto. Why the city insists on calling it Runnymede Park we'll never know, but still, when we went last year, they were getting ready to flood the ice rinks. The boards were up. One set of boards would form the cushion for the guys to play hockey, the other one is just for fun. Junior played hockey with Big Rep on the hockey rink and skated around with me on the other. Boy, we had lots of fun in that old park. We sat looking at the trees when a screeching train pulled along the siding that separates the park from Redfern's backyard. Running past the fences on Cobalt and out towards the St. Clair plants, they made quite a racket. Once the train pulled north of St. Clair, things quieted down. But God, you know, if smells were sounds, the stench of fear, fresh meat and dung would be like an atomic bomb. You notice Princess Elizabeth didn't stop by for a tour of the stockyards? Junior and I were going to leave that disaster of a neighbourhood. We joked that we lived in an even worse place than in Strangers on a Train."

"I know, Crissie, I know. But right now, I need to learn anything you know about what Junior was doing on the 30th. It's important. Anything you can remember, even if it doesn't seem important, might help us find out who killed Junior," I stared right into her blue eyes.

"All I know is that he was going to collect off a packing house worker who lived on Ryding Avenue, across the street from our park. And he never came back."

AND THE PEOPLE START TO SING —AL'S VERSION

I left the Double R and the old man I wanted to talk to was anxiously waiting to board the streetcar that was already pulled up in front of Guffin's Hardware. He had been around the neighbourhood for a long time and worked as a handler at Dufferin Race Track. We exchanged nods of recognition and I motioned to him to get on and followed. We sat near the back and because it was a little early for the downtown workers to begin their morning trek, we had some privacy.

I didn't have to prompt him.

"We owed Junior O from a couple of bad bets I'd made and he agreed to forget the money when we offered to give him a sure-thing tip. The only catch was that I had to lay sizable bets down for him with a number of bookies of my acquaintance. He gave me the money to wager and I collected a day or two after the race and turned the money over to Junior. That's the strange part."

He took a deep breath. "The bookies in the city loan money to one another, at reasonable rates, so they can cover bets when they get hit hard. If you have to go outside your own circle of friends you're going to be dealing with a loan shark and rates are pretty stiff. Having hit a lot of bookies hard anonymously, and with anonymous bets, Junior then openly loaned them the money at loan shark rates and accepted repayment in installments."

"10 per cent a week or part thereof?" I ventured.

"Or worse," he said. "You pay the bet and the vigorish at the end of the week. If you can't get it up, you pay the interest. You get away with that for a couple of weeks, maybe three or four, and then the rate goes up. Junior borrowed a very large amount at low or no interest—

from some family member, probably his mother—which he re-loaned to the bookies at usurious rates."

At that point the lyrics of Ace in the Hole ran through my head once more. A lot louder when I got to the part Some folks write to the old folks for coin. It was starting to come together.

We had reached the point where he had to change streetcars to get to work so we split. He had been helpful and said he would be available if I had any more questions. I had a number of questions but not for him so I headed back to the Junction. I got off the streetcar at the end of the line to find Cappie waiting in front of the Long Store.

"He's in Dempsey's," he said anticipating my wanting to talk to Norbert O.

"And Kat is waiting for you at the Mission," he concluded.

I headed for the Mission where she was waiting for me, knowing I would want a truthful explanation. It seemed an appropriate setting.

"When he was killed, as near as I can make out, there were seven bookies who still owed Junior O sizable amounts. Amounts that represented the balance of the loans he had made to them over a year ago. What a gas! He knows the race is rigged so he gets a bunch of nobodies to make large bets with a whole bunch of bookies using money he provides. Very few of them are able to pay it off right away and Junior uses every cent he has, and some he borrows from his brothers, to make loans to the bookies at big interest so that they can pay off the bets. As they get paid off, the nobodies turn the money over to Junior who has made a big bundle on the race and afterwards was making a bundle on the loans, although that was getting smaller and smaller as loans were paid off."

"So what went wrong?" I asked.

"Some smart ass bookie eager to pay off his loan tried to give the cash to Izzy who naturally asked questions and the obliging bookie told him about his loan. By that time, everybody and his brother knew that a bunch of jockeys had rigged a race and were in trouble because of it. So Izzy suspected Junior of being involved in that one loan and acted accordingly. He had no idea that there were a lot of other bookies who had been taken by his dear brother Junior. Izzy had filled Norbert in. Being a decent sort, Nobby quietly kept collecting for his dead brother, and turning the money over to me for delivery to the preacher and the young widow. Once he started doing this he realized that there was a lot more money involved than he and Izzy knew"

"Nobby sincerely regretted the family schism. He was seriously concerned about Crissie's well being and the poor baby who had lost his father. With Norbert, being an uncle was a special loving thing." She had tears in her eyes as she finished the story and I gave her my handkerchief which got me a very warm smile.

"I'm worried about Izzy," she confessed. "I don't think he realizes there is still some money coming in and once he finds out he will not let it get funnelled to Crissie. Can you do anything?"

"Leave it with me," I said, without explaining that I didn't understand why I should now be expected to tell one son-of-a-bitch to let the other son-of-a-bitch collect the third son-of-a-bitch's loans. We signed on to find out who murdered that third brother. Sticking to that without deviation seemed to make good sense.

I stuck my head into Dempsey's where Nobby was nursing a cup of coffee and his head. He looked me straight in the eye. I told him to keep the money flowing. We'd talk later and I left.

I walked east on the north side of Dundas and as I approached Keele Street, turned into the Alps restaurant. Cappie was there sipping what was supposedly iced tea. Tired as he was, his usual smile lit up his corner of the world and, as it invariably did, made me chuckle.

"How goes it?" he said.

"Who the hell killed Junior O?" I asked, very frustrated, which I knew was par for the course.

"We did this bit already. You know! You're the private eye! You tell me who dunnit!" He was enjoying this.

I was frustrated. The private eye business was always frustrating. Well, maybe Will or Red will come through.

I ordered a Crisp Vegetable Sandwich and a glass of milk. Cappie almost choked on an ice cube. I thought that after lunch I would walk down to the Annette Street Library and in that quiet environment think things through and maybe, just maybe, come up with something.

A COLD NIGHT WITH A PURPLE SKY—RED'S VERSION

After Crissie left with my handkerchief, and a promise of keeping in touch, I sprinted up Simpson's back stairs to Yonge Street. Past the construction, I just barely caught the Dundas streetcar. 25 minutes later at Annette; I left the warmth of the streetcar headed for the public library. I missed having a library around the corner, for its books, magazines and coziness. Up the steps and through the front door, I headed to the reference section for the city directories. It took a bit of time, but I cross referenced the street numbers on Ryding Avenue with the names of the people, and their occupations, who lived on the street. Don Little, at 282 Ryding, was the only one listed as an abitior worker. Hmm, he owned the house too. I wrote down the number and address in my little book. Good bet that's the guy Junior collected, or tried to collect from on his final night.

I wished Will was with me so we could duck across the tracks as Crissie described and pick up a lead or two. I borrowed the telephone from the librarian who had more than a touch of an Edinburgh brogue, Anne was her name, and called the Metropole on the chance Will might be there. It was a sad realization that I had committed the telephone number of a beer hall to memory. Bruno said Will hadn't been in the hall today and neither had Al. On a whim, I dialed our office phone. The phone rang and predictably went unanswered. With the phone back in its cradle, I turned and literally bumped into Al.

We excitedly exchanged news of our morning 'til the shushers shooed us out of the library. Wouldn't you know, as we headed up Pacific Avenue towards Vine Avenue, Nikov was coming down from Dundas and hailed Al. Man to man, they conferred while I stood meekly furious off to the side.

"Izzy was following Junior," Al confided as we left Nikov and continued our march to Vine. "Chaim saw Junior being followed by Izzy. Chaim left the junkyard and was out on the tracks, looking at the sky in the early evening. Chaim was watching a strange sunset with lightning and thunder. He saw Junior wearing his working clothes, a black knit cap and pea jacket, and then saw Izzy keeping low, but definitely trailing Junior across the tracks. Don't know why Chaim didn't tell me last week, maybe he didn't think it was important or didn't place it on the night of the murder."

"What was it you told me a while back? Use the old fashion techniques, look for motive and look for opportunity. Izzy certainly has the motive to murder Junior, inheriting money and protecting the family business. But we still don't know how and when."

"Maybe our man Little will help us find out how," Al replied while walking fast towards the hole in the chain link fence. We dodged a few slow moving trains on the tracks and ran between. A signal man yelled at us, but Al yelled back, "Give it up Harry. Us chickens are just trying to get to the other side."

Harry yelled back with an entirely different tone, "Make it quick Al, you ain't supposed to be on the tracks. You'll get me in a heap of trouble one of these days."

And I thought I grew up in a small town.

Once across the tracks, we ducked into the auto repair shop, onto West Toronto Street and along Dods to Ryding Avenue. For a short while, we stood leaning against a tree in Ryding Park looking towards 282 Ryding Avenue. The boards were up in the park for the flooding of the rink cushions, much as Crissie described. 282 was a tidy little house with white curtains drawn to precisely the same height in the window frame. The lawn was sharply cut and cleanly raked with a naked pruned rose vine pinned tightly to the white trellis by the front door. Looked like the walks had been swept at least twice today. This kind of tidy usually meant someone had a need for control. I figure we got the right house.

Ignoring the front door, Al made a bee line for the side door and rapped hard twice when he arrived. I heard a woman with a cockney accent call from within the house, "Who's there?" The door opened a sliver. Again," Who's there?"

"Al Green and my associate, Dotty Brophy." I might have imagined her sneer and narrowed eyes at the surname, but no matter, Al had this one. "We're investigating the death of Junior O and would like a word with your husband, Hank Little, if we may."

"He's sleeping. He works the nights. He doesn't know anything about no O," Mrs. Little, we presume, replied.

The next door neighbour's side door opened. A tall large man, looked like a CP worker, stared at us, then at the presumed Mrs. Little and said with a Scottish brogue, "Mabel, these people here bothering you?"

"They want Don but he's sleeping. Something about that bookie's son who was murdered," Mabel Little said in a whisper, probably not to waken her husband.

The neighbour said, "He wouldn't know anything about any dirty business I can assure you. He's an honest working man."

After Al introduced himself, we learned the neighbour's name was Haines. I noted that Al did not introduce me this time.

Al said, "I'm sure Mr. Little is an honest hard working man. No doubt in my mind. But something happened about three weeks ago in the early evening. We're trying to figure out what. Did anything unusual happen at the end of October that you can recall?"

"Well, yes, Mr. Green, something unusual did. My wife called for a constable," he said proudly. "Some hobo holed up in the Little's backyard. Don and I chased him, but he charged right through Mabel's vegetable garden and hiked himself over the fence. Spry, he was. Hard to see him, he was all dressed in black. We think he banged his leg because we heard a crash and he swore some. Don and I debated climbing the fence, but ran around to Cobalt and up the tracks to cut him off in the lane. We lost him. He must of cleared the waist high picket fence, and tripped over little Joan's tricycle — we figure he tripped over because the tricycle was on its side, and passed between the wee houses out onto St. Clair."

"Don and I chased him and Mabel ran along too. We were lucky the constables were sitting by the call box at Runnymede, so they were here in no time. Don and I waved the constables down. One was quite a young chap. Earnest lad. We steered them towards the school and over to Britannia. Mabel here thought he had a knife and told them so too."

I imagined the conversation sounded like one in a pub somewhere in England. I guessed Mr. Haine's young chap is Number Nine's newest recruit, Constable Daniel Old.

Mr. Haines continued, "They told us to go home. A minute later, I heard shouting. 'Stop! Police! Throw out your weapon! Toronto Police.' A minute later, I hear a couple of gun shots. But when they came around, the officers said that they lost the hobo to York county at the fence at the end of Britannia. They advised us to lock our doors and windows and to call if he came back. We did the right thing, they said."

"Anything else?" Al said after letting out a long whistle.

"No, no. He has not been back. We taught him what for!" Mr. Haines said.

Al thanked them, gave each a card and advised a message could be left at the Double R if they thought of anything else. As we left I said, "Top of the day to ya." Al looked sideways at me before we walked west towards Runnymede. He was quiet about the quip.

"Looks like Old shot at Junior. Old mentioned this when I met with him, but I'll pass by Number Nine now. But Al, really, why anyone would think that hobos are people who dress in black is beyond me."

Al laughed. "Yes, but no mention of our boy Izzy. He probably watched from the park and stayed back. Have a talk with Old. I'll meet you at the Metropole when you're done."

The detective was in and we met in the same dreary room as before.

"Miss Brophy, how's your investigation proceeding?"

"Well. How's yours proceeding?" I replied.

He looked puzzled. "Well . . . you must understand the complexities of the competing demands between the station and headquarters."

"I know, I know. Bank robbers breaking out of the Don, Princess touring the city, kid's bike renewing and all that jazz. But, tell me, what about the call on Ryding Avenue three weeks ago? Wanna know why I'm asking? My associates and I suspect the hobo you chased to York county was Junior O."

Now Old looks puzzled. "Let me get my notes."

Old oddly showed his notes to me, a small notebook with pages covered by a wide loopy scrawl.

Headed south on Runnymede from the call box on the north side of St. Clair Avenue West and then east on Ryding Avenue. Employed siren. Mrs. Haines at 280 Ryding Avenue advised her husband and neighbour, Mr. Little, had chased the suspect from the rear yard of 282 Ryding up Cobalt Avenue to St. Clair Avenue West. Two citizens in the middle of St. Clair. Advised by Mrs. Little, who joined Mr. Haines and Mr. Little, that suspect was armed with a weapon (knife). As per witnesses' statements, suspect may have fled the scene on Britannia Avenue or through the St. Clair Avenue Public School yard.

Advised citizens to return to their homes.

Proceeded on foot westerly along St. Clair Avenue West. Inspected schoolyard and garden. No sign of suspect. Proceeded on foot westerly on St. Clair and northerly on Britannia Avenue. Streetlight out at the end of the street. We witnessed some movement at the dead end near the fence. After verbal warnings with the citizen report of the suspect being armed, my partner fired two shots towards the fence. Further investigation revealed no blood or clear sighting of suspect. Partner advised the fence at the dead end of Britannia Avenue marked the boundary between the City of Toronto and the County of York.

Returned to Ryding Avenue to interview citizens. Suspect was loitering in the rear yard of Mr. Don and Mabel Little's house at 282 Ryding Avenue. As per witness statements, suspect was medium height, slight build and wore dark clothing. Interrupted and pursued by Mr. Don Little and Mr. Elliot Haines after the suspect fled over back fence. Inspected rear yard. Advised by citizens that hobos come up from the train tracks on occasion, though irregularly in recent years.

Returned to Runnymede call box to advise Headquarters to alert the York County Police.

Returned to Number Nine Station at 8:45 pm.

"Did you ever hear of a hobo all dressed in black?" I asked. "Mr. Haines told Al and I the guy was spry and all dressed in black with a black knit hat. Sounds like the same guy that was seen crossing the tracks that night. Oh, yeah. By the way, Junior wore a black pea jacket and wool cap when he was collecting."

Old shook his head. "Well, I'll be darned."

METROPOLE SUMMIT NUMBER SIX—AL'S VERSION

Red and I arrived at the Metropole almost simultaneously. Will was already there, but I couldn't tell for how long. It had been a long hard day for all.

Will jumped in first. He was justifiably pleased with himself for the progress he had made with Mrs. O at the ballet. In particular he was chuffed by the fact that he had, on hearing that she was one of the executors of Junior's estate, been able to tactfully learn that Kat and the preacher were also executors.

There was a pause while John delivered our food orders. I was hungry and looked at my dinner with anticipation. Somewhere under that puddle of gravy was a slice of meatloaf. Two mounds of greyish white, white mashed potatoes guarded my dinner on the left, a mountain of fresh out-of-the-can peas guarded the right. I attacked from the front and barely noticed that

Will was having his usual plain burger with nothing on it, just a bun and slab of fried ground meat. Red had her favourite, fish and chips.

Red was not above talking with her mouth full and was anxious to continue the conversation. Will's report about the estate executors had energized her recall, and she blurted out the fact that Izzy and Nobby were the residual beneficiaries. If Crissie and Josh passed away at the same time as Junior, or within thirty days of Junior's death, Izzy and Nobby would collect the entire estate. The fact that this would mean that the girl and her baby were in considerable danger wasn't mitigated by the notion that the brothers might not have any knowledge of the provisions of Junior's will. After all, their mother was one of the executors.

While it could be implied that the motive for Junior's murder was money, the root of all evil, we could not explain the attempt to cover up his being choked by firing the gunshots into his body. While we didn't know where the murder had taken place, we were reasonably sure it was not in Winnipeg. Even the sound of the shots emanating in the Ryding Avenue area could not be looked at as helpful. Junior was a lightweight, but carrying or dragging the body the considerable distance to the meat packing plant's loading dock would have been difficult. We knew the body had to have been put in the freight car at the plant as the customary tin seal, which was threaded through the catch on the huge doors, was still intact when they prepared to open the doors in Winnipeg. He must have been killed closer to the ice house.

While not entirely sure of the whereabouts of Crissie

and Josh, we knew they were in serious danger as they stood between Izzy and Nobby, and Junior's substantial estate. If we attached ourselves to the two brothers, possibly as a rotating stakeout, we would effectively protect the girl and her child.

This being our agreed plan of action, we decided it would have to be an early night to ensure that we got an early start. On that note, we signaled Bruno to draw us a couple of long ones each so we could toast our endeavours of the morrow.

NOVEMBER 20, 1951
I DON'T LIKE SURPRISES—AL'S VERSION

We met at our office in the Sterling Tower at nine Tuesday morning. We debated the merits of taking a taxi while walking north on Bay Street, past City Hall where our debate ended as we were looking into the eyes of a TTC motorman who smiled at Red like they knew each other. Apparently they did because she called him Frank. He extended his hand, covering the fare box, indicating that we were getting a free ride. Red chatted with him for a minute, while Will and I moved on to the back of the car.

The day was starting off well. The streetcar was almost completely empty so we had the rear of the rocket to ourselves. We rehashed the discussion of the previous night and talked about our responsibility. We were hired to determine who murdered Junior O. We did not have to get physical with anyone. We needed only to prove that Izzy killed his brother, which in our hearts, we knew was true. We had laughed over beer about the radio shows making big things out of "motive, means, and opportunity," and chuckled at our collective inability to come up with anything clear-cut that matched even one of the three. We were doing what we had agreed we had to do. We were going to confront the brothers O and being as accusingly abrasive as possible, provoke a reaction which we hoped would blow the lid off the case.

When we reached the Double R, George had fresh coffee poured for us; we had savoured the aroma as we came in the door. Red, of course, ordered a tea. He was too busy to join us, but when he had a chance for a breather we exchanged pleasantries with George, who remarked on how unusual it was for all three of us to grace his establishment simultaneously, particularly with the O boys so close by. With what seemed like a casual comment, he had our attention.

"Where are they?" demanded Red.

"In the bank." said George, "They were in here for a while waiting for the bank to open. The three of them were quite jovial."

"The three of them?" questioned a surprised Will.

"Yah," George said, "Izzy, Nobby, and Cappie."

I was surprised to hear that Cappie had been here in the company of the bad guys and that he apparently had gone with them to the bank. I didn't like the sound of this at all. It raised more questions than it answered. The three of us were on our feet quickly and, as we headed out, I dropped a deuce on the counter next to the cash register to more than cover the cost of everything we had guzzled in the last couple of weeks.

We moved past Guffin's Hardware store and a few steps further, stepped through the doors of the Imperial Bank on the corner. They were in the line waiting for one of the tellers to become available, but turned to face us as we poured through the door. They hadn't expected us and were not overjoyed at our presence. I looked Cappie in the eye. He wasn't smiling this morning; in fact, he looked a few years older as a result of the stress he must have been under, as he had plumbed my stupid brain for information that would be of interest to his associates. The fact that Red, Will and I had worked independently, updating each other regularly but not discussing our associates' interests or progress with others, had made it impossible for him to keep track of what was happening except with dumbass Al.

"It looks like we got here in the nick of time!" I said. They were nonplussed.

"Checking the bank balance to see if you've got enough to warrant knocking off the broad and her kid?" I came right out with it, right there in the bank and loud enough to ensure that everyone heard what I had said.

"Shut up!" snarled Izzy. He had produced a pistol from under his sling.

I slid the Police Positive out of my pocket and pointed it at Izzy. He didn't seem to be impressed, but the pressure was telling on him and I noted the saliva slowly trickling from one corner of his mouth.

"You're in over your head," he said, and continued, "I know how to use mine and you haven't got a bloody clue."

He was right, of course, but there was no backing

down. I decided to add more pressure; he was ready to crack.

"The only person you ever shot was your brother and he was already dead when that happened, wasn't he?" I gave it all I had.

"You can't prove anything," said Izzy, gradually losing confidence.

Red spoke out, "We can prove enough to show what it really is."

Red produced the Iver Johnson from her bag. "You're outnumbered. Drop the gun."

She must have slipped back to the office last night and picked up the original office gun. Smart move. It wasn't going to do us any good lying at the bottom of a desk drawer.

"Now . . . don't shoot anybody . . ." said Cappie, the cherubic smile back on his face and his white teeth gleaming. "You're a sweet girl and it would be hard for you to live with the fact that you used a gun and hurt somebody." He was slowly inching toward Red, who was standing feet wide with both arms locked straight and hands on the pistol. I was sure that when he got close enough, he would make a grab for the gun.

Then it happened.

It was a hell of a bang!

Red shot him!

The bullet hit him in the upper arm, smashed the humerus, continued on through him and lodged in Nobby's thigh. Nobby did not seem to be in any pain, but Cappie was on the floor making terrible noises. There was a lot of blood and even a couple of shards of splintered bone sticking out through the sleeve of his suit jacket.

Someone hit the alarm button. It started to ring loudly, and after a rather short interlude you could hear the wail of an annoying police siren.

Will picked up an ink stand off the counter. It didn't have any ink in the inkwell and it didn't have a pen. It wasn't nailed down because nobody wanted to steal an empty inkstand. Izzy crumpled to the floor unconscious as a result of getting one upside the head with that empty inkstand.

I glanced over at the clerk in charge of the vault. It was Penny Nichols. We knew each other and I think she knew what I had in mind. Izzy's pistol was on the floor so I scooped it up, took the Iver Johnson from Red and walked swiftly to the gate in the counter which Penny obligingly opened. As we entered the vault, I gave Penny the key to my father's big safety deposit box. It was almost empty. I dumped the three weapons in the box and she had it back in place in seconds. She didn't bother have me sign the access card or to give me my key as I'd get that and the guns back later too. I took the same spot in the group that I had left only seconds before. Red had a very black look on her face.

"Don't let it bother you," I said. "You did the right thing."

"But," she said, "I was aiming for the centre of the blur from only a couple of feet away; I was way off and hit him in the arm." She wasn't oozing sympathy.

"You need a little practice," I said which was the only thing I could think to say.

In the meantime, people had fled the bank but not too far, as they didn't want to miss any excitement. Will, knowing how the police operated, slowly walked Nobby outside, walking beside him in such a way as to conceal the bullet hole in his leg. He wasn't bleeding very much, possibly because the bullet had just penetrated the flesh. One of Blore's Taxis was waiting outside for a possible passenger. They have a sort of second sense about when they will be needed. It's weird.

Will handed the taxi driver a piece of bank stationery on which he had written the name and address of a downtown doctor, an indecipherable message which contained instructions to avoid reporting the accidental wounding to the police, and to charge Nobby accordingly. Will mingled with the swelling crowd with the intention of playing the agitator should crowd support be necessary. He was sporting a rare look of satisfaction as he was not a fan of the Toronto constabulary and knew they would spend great amounts of time looking for the missing bullet.

The police arrived, led into the bank by Dorothy's favourite flatfoot Constable Daniel Old, looking very officious. For some reason I felt like snickering and Red was similarly affected. A little bit of the pressure was off and I think that had something to do with it. The bank staff couldn't answer any questions about what had happened, they were all hiding at the time. Old demanded that I produce my weapon and I thought Red was going to burst out laughing. He didn't really believe that I did not have a gun but my jacket was wide open and the telltale signs that usually indicate the presence of a concealed weapon were not evident.

"What happened here?" Old demanded of Red.

"I don't know, Constable," lied Red.

"Was this an attempted bank robbery?" Old speculated.

"Yes! Yes! Bravo officer! He's one of the Boyd gang!" came a voice from the crowd that sounded more than a little familiar.

"Where is his gun?" demanded Old.

"I think the one who left before you got here took it," said Penny Nichols who had sensed the propensity of the group to pull Old's tail.

"No! No!" said a chorus from the crowd outside, but nothing by way of direction was forthcoming with the denial.

"Who shot this man?" It was a different voice, Sergeant Sullivan from Number Nine.

The ambulance attendants had lifted Cappie on to a stretcher but Sullivan held them up.

"Who shot you son?" asked a solicitous Sullivan.

"I don't know, sir," whispered Cappie. Another who was familiar with police tactics.

"Did you see someone with a gun?" encouraged Sullivan.

"No sir!" was the response of an almost comatose Cappie.

"Who shot this man?" demanded Old as well, loud enough that answers were likely to come from persons some distance away.

"I did," said a polite female voice.

It was Mrs. O.

"He murdered my son; I shot him," she said bluntly and produced a revolver from her shoulder bag.

Sullivan ordered Old to arrest Mrs. O and call for a female constable to take her into custody.

Eventually the charges against her were dropped. The revolver had never been fired and there was some doubt that Cappie had been shot in the bank as the bullet had never been found. Cappie was charged with attempted bank robbery but charges were dropped due to lack of evidence.

At the first opportunity, Red, Will and I had jumped on a streetcar and headed for the Metropole. We sat at the rear of the almost empty car and had gone about six or seven blocks before we howled with laughter.

AFTERWORD
JUNIOR–IZZY'S VERSION

Junior's dumber than even I thought. Always was and now always will be. He just never thought things through right. Like the old man wouldn't hear he had a jockey in his pocket. Old Slide Slim came straight to my old man because Slim knows what side his bread gets buttered. And what does Junior do with his stolen loaf? Sent it to the stupid Irish girl and her bastard son. And hell, using that old mission windbag who paraded the brown envelope all the way down Maria Street to the side door of the shul. The ceremonious walk like he was King George. All the old ladies on Maria yapping. Junior broke my mother's heart. Great scheme, Junior.

Junior didn't even twig I was following until I stepped in the hole by a tree in Ryding Park. I stayed pressed flat against a tree. He looked around but he didn't check around. Dumb.

After the Ryding neighbours chased him, I was worried that the cops might grab him. That would be bad for the old man's business. To give him time to get away, I threw an old coat at the county fence—cops with their hair trigger fingers shot at the bloody thing. Afterwards, catching up to him through the bush and the field up near the Symes Incinerator, I taught Junior what's what. Maybe I don't have a girlfriend and bastard son but I couldn't take being doubted. I knocked him down for that one, knelt on his chest and strangled the life out of him. After finishing him off, I shot him twice in the gut. Worst comes to worst, the cops take the blame. I dumped the dumb buck in an open refrigerated car near the ice house. Who's a big man now, eh, Junior? Dumped—he's somebody's problem now, not ours. Like I say, dumb.

Acknowledgements

Many thanks to our entire family for their example and inspiration. Appreciation in particular is extended to Dorothy and Albert Newton, Margaret and Frank Ball, Joan and Frank Ball, Anne Newton, George Comninel and Daniel Young.

Along the way, friends, acquaintances and supporters cheered us through and provided their support: Lynn Crosbie; Joe Fiorito of the Toronto Star; Kristjan Harris and Amelia Laidlaw of Saving Gigi Cafe; Michael Holmes; Luciano Icoabelli of Quattro Books; Bruno Marchese; Rahna Moreau, Liane McLarty of Ryerson University's The Eyeopener, Marcello Musto, Corrado Paina, Lisa Rainford of The Villager; and Angie Swartz.

In addition, Ken Newton would like to thank Dan Dimitroff and Peter Copeman: friends of my youth with whom I shared some hilarious and some serious times, which are now the subject of exaggeration at our Wednesday get-togethers for medium double-doubles. They supplied the bits and pieces of trivia that had escaped my feeble memory.

The Toronto Public Library system was an invaluable resource for our research. Through their Writer In Residence Program, Shawn Micallef and Marina Endicott provided kind and wise professional advice as did numerous librarians. In particular, we thank Cynthia Fisher of the Humanities and Social Sciences Section at the Toronto Reference Library.

We are indebted to course director Michael O'Connor and the talented students of York University's Professional Writing Program: Catherine Belvedere, James Douglas David Applewhaite, Amanda Black, Zunera Buttar, Laura Granger, Cameron L. Hardy, Alex Harvey, Tashrifa Hossain, Alissa Rothman, James Karcza, Talia Leacock, Christie Maragos, Victoria Mattacchione, Celeste Miller, Ameera Mohammed, Paisley Pasloske, Holly Penick, Elodie Quetant, Danielle Staring, Jamie Tabug, and Wyshnavy Yogeswaran. Leaping Lion Books is the best collaborative publisher for the three of us who wrote Junction Book.

None of the aforementioned people, of course, are responsible for whatever problems arise in the book.

Once again, we sincerely thank all of those who contributed to the memories herein recalled.